TO BE THE BEST
"The Story Of Johnny Powers"

BY JOE DOLAN

DEDICATION

To Master Choe who influenced my life for the positive.

Chapter 1

Let me take you back in time a little. I'd like to introduce you to the sport of WARRIOR FIGHTING. It pre-dates all the mixed martial art cage fighting programs on TV today, but it's very similar to what you are familiar with. Call it the Grandfather of MMA.

The story you'll read is really a tale about one of the sport's most renowned fighters, Johnny Powers. He was a local kid, maybe just like you, but he had a spark. In a world where the common athlete in the sport was concerned with how big his arms were or how hard he could hit, Johnny was a little different. He cared about honor and somehow it seems, honor cared back.

We're going to a city you may know of, but for the sake of the story we'll call it Metropolis. You'll get a fix on when this all happened as you read his story.

It was all about the cities best competition for Martial Arts styled, 'anything goes' fighting. From one side of the televised arena to the other you would find winners and losers making bets and taking risks they couldn't afford. The kind of risks that could make or break your wallet and there was money in the room for every fight.

Since the Warrior Fights hit prime time television, the seats in the arena had been filled to capacity. Corporate sponsors paid a small fortune for thirty seconds of air time and homes throughout Metropolis tuned in week after week to find out who was the best at this sport of kings.

In the center of the arena, surrounded by camera crews and throngs of people yelling, stood a regulation sized boxing ring. There was no ordinary boxing in this ring however, Warrior Fights was so much more than boxing. In the Warrior Fights ring, the rule was to literally kill or be killed, or at least to knock out or be knocked out . In Metropolis, this is where the real action was!

At either side of the squared circle stood two angry looking figures dressed in leather and chains. They had built their skills up to face off in what promised to be a top draw beat down.

To the left was a competition worthy Warrior Fights contender by the name of *Tiger*. Dressed in black and orange striped ring pants and a bright orange Lucha libre mask, indicative of the W.F.C. style of dress, Tiger was no stranger to the sport of extreme fighting. He had been a top contender in this arena for the past year since he won his first match. He had since fought against some of the best up and coming fighters in the sport and he donned a new chain on his leather vest with each fight he won. Suffice to say, his vest was well covered in silver.

Squaring off with Tiger and impatiently bouncing up and down on his toes was a sort of new-comer to the Warrior Fights program. A towering 6 foot and 4 inch tall behemoth known by the name of Fist. Recognized for his stone hard knuckles and fast working hands, Fist earned his nick-name, his grey fighter mask and the chance to square off with Tiger by winning his last seven televised matches. His most recent win was due to a colossal knockout blow at the 13 second mark in the first round of the fight. Tonight, he hoped to do the same against Tiger.

The starting bell rang and brought the crowd to their feet. As the two warriors met in the middle of the ring the scuffle began.

The spectators in the audience were always of a mixed breed. Some wore suits and ties and others were dressed in jeans and t-shirts. The arena sold general admission tickets to the weekly televised broadcast, allowing for first come and first served seating. This meant that the sooner you arrived at the ticket booth then the better your choice of seating was. This allowed the common working man to have as good of a view of the fight as the high rollers who were in attendance. No matter who you were, if you had money to spend you could bet it on the spill of blood at the Warrior Fights Arena.

There were a series of *Ooh's* and *Aah's* as Tiger got tossed into the turnbuckle at the start of the match. Dwarfed by the towering size of Fist, it appeared that Tiger was at a disadvantage. Never-the-less, he recovered quickly and rushed back in with an attack. Fist connected again with a wide right hook to Tiger's left check, but this time it did little to stun him.

Tiger shook it off and taunted Fist saying, "Is that all you've got big boy?" He stood with his arms open and laughed.

Fist brought around another wide armed punch but it was deflected by Tiger as he responded with a flurry of rabbit punches to the head and body of Fist. Tiger stepped back and jumped in the air, delivering a shocking and lighting quick kick to Fist's sternum. It was so powerful that it sent Fist stumbling back into the ropes at the edge of the ring. It seemed clear that Tiger struck a damaging blow with the kick. Hanging over the top rope in disarray and now facing a group of rowdy teenagers in the front row, Fist reached down and outside of the ring. He retrieved a conveniently placed pine 2x4 that lay across a ringside table

One of the teen-aged spectators in the front row called out to him screaming, "Kill him Fist! Kill him!"

Overlooking the arena was the W.F.C. Headquarters Home Office. Chairman and League Owner Gary Grasier watched the match with his partner Sheila White, sitting in a big bay window. He leaned in toward Sheila with his arms crossed and quietly pointed her attention to the match.

"Watch how good they make this look," he told her, pointing with his elbow.

Down in the ring Fist turned back to face his opponent. Swinging over the top of his head he brought the 2x4 down like an axe toward Tiger's bright orange head. Tiger raised a left forearm block in a quick upward motion and the board snapped on contact with his leather cuff. Splinters flew and the force of the blow brought Tiger down to one knee.

Throwing aside a piece of the pine that was still in his hand, Fist loomed over Tiger with his threatening presence. Ready to strike again, he was taken off guard as Tiger jumped up in a bounding push from the mat. Tiger delivered an open palm strike to Fist's jaw-line. The impact made Fist's legs weak and wobbly. As his body began to fall limp, Tiger grabbed him at the neck and hip and hoisted him high into the air.

With an effortless toss, he ejected Fist from the ring and down onto the table where the 2x4 was found. The table collapsed under the pressure and left Fist unconscious on his back. The audience showered him with popcorn buckets and crumpled up betting slips with his name on them. That was all they were good after his loss. The fight went to Tiger! He walked the inside of the ring, taunting the objectors and pointing to the fans that cheered him on.

The spectators went wild. One yelled out, "Atta-Boy Tiger, you just made me a mint!"

Upstairs Sheila smiled at the display in the ring. This kind of action was keeping Warrior Fights in the top television slot on Channel Five's Monday night line-up and the results meant money.

"They made that look so real I would have bet on it myself," she said.

Gary turned to Sheila and gave her a peck on the lips.

"Sheila," he affirmed, "with these morons throwing their money away, you'll never have to."

Gary sprang to his feet and made his way down the staircase from the office door to the aisle by the ring. He climbed inside and stepped up next to Tiger who was still growling and grunting at the crowd. He raised the winner's hand over his head. Using the wireless microphone in his other hand he addressed the crowd.

"Put your hands together for Tiger! A top contender for a title match at this year's Rumble Royale!"

The audience responded with cheers. Tiger took another moment to enjoy the cheering before making his way out of the ring, leaving Gary and the referee inside. Gary talked to the masses both in the room and through the TV cameras.

"We're going to take a commercial break and let some of our guests get their bets in for the big match of the night. Remember that you viewers at home have up to one minute before the match to place your bets online, so grab those credit cards and log on now. We'll be back in five!"

Gary held a pointing finger at the TV camera as the red light on top shut off.

"It's a cut," the camera man said.

Gary turned from the camera and handed the microphone to the referee and rushed back up the staircase to the office where Sheila stood waiting.

"This is one of the best crowds we've had yet. I can smell the money," she said, grabbing Gary in her arms.

Gary smiled in agreement. He said, "Our TV show has

made street fighting the sport for the common man. Every punk fighter in Metropolis wants a piece of the action and anyone with an ounce of talent thinks he's got what it takes to compete with our boys."

"Well," Sheila said, "you would have to agree that our boys are the best."

"That's right!" Gary laughed. "The best actors money can buy!"

Sheila smiled with a wink as Gary picked up and gulped down a glass of wine. The next fighters were heading toward the ring.

In the crowd, the excitement was building. The big match of the night was about to begin! A stunning and well dressed pair of high rollers took their seats at ringside.

"This is the one we came for honey," the wife said.

"You know it babe," the husband replied. "This is better than a trip to Vegas."

Lights flashed overhead to signal the end of betting and the spectators scrambled back to their seats.

A single fighter walked the mat inside the ring. Ripped and ready for action, he taunted the crowd from inside the ropes.

Gary's voice came over the speakers and the cameras came alive.

"Now, ladies and gentlemen. For the thousands in attendance and the millions tuned in on Channel Five, it's the fight you've been waiting to see."

A hush settled over the crowd.

"You've seen him on billboards all over Metropolis. You've watched him on Monday Night's biggest fights and tonight you'll see him in action. Here he is, the former champion of the W.F.C. – Blade!

The circling spotlights in the room focused on a set of double doors at the back of the arena. Through the rising smoke from the fog machines, the doors burst open with the kick of a giant red leather boot. Blade's enormous body followed through the door and the crowd erupted in screams, whistles and cheers.

A Story By Joe Dolan

Chapter 2

The downtown Metropolis of today didn't feature the same *Golden Mile* that in the past made this city great. What was a string of a dozen blocks bustling with retail shops and restaurants had been reduced to a garment district, some liquor stores and a few low rent apartment buildings. In the middle of what was once a shopper's paradise now stood the last remaining store on the block. Huon's General Store.

It hadn't opened for business yet, it was still early. All of the shelves were neatly organized and fully stocked for the locals to do their shopping. The aisles were swept clean, mopped and ready for business. The lights were still out though and the 'closed' sign was waiting to be turned to 'open'.

From a room in the back of the store, a cone of light pierced the dark sales floor. If you had walked in you would have heard the sounds of kicks and strikes making contact with focus pads and sandbags. Between those strikes and blows, the shadow of a fighter crossed back and forth in the halogen light.

That fighter was Johnny Powers. A strapping young nineteen-year-old with his head in the clouds and his mind on his art. He arrived at work a good two hours early every morning so he could practice his Tae Kwon Do.

In the back room, Johnny had set up a series of sandbags that hung from the rafters. He lined the walls with wooden targets and arranged focus pads to practice his strikes and kicks on. It was a gym he'd constructed just for himself.

Johnny was swift and powerful, but he was confronted by his limitations. He wanted to jump higher, hit harder and perform better. He strived to reach these goals by working to improve his technique every single day.

Johnny grabbed a box from the floor. He threw it into the air and leapt off the ground, spinning and kicking the box through the air like a tournament soccer player. Pleased with this, he picked up a tennis ball and attempted to do the same. With all of his effort, he spun around and landed a perfect 360 degree spin-kick, but he missed the ball. The ball dropped to the floor, even before his high kick had landed, but still – he didn't make contact with it. He caught it on the first bounce and turned to throw it in frustration.

Before he completed that angry toss he saw the outline of a Chinese figure, mid-fifties and five and a half feet tall in the doorway. It was his boss and friend, Lap Huon.

"Another early morning for Johnny Powers?" Lap questioned.

"Yes Mr. Huon. You know I have to work out every day to get stronger and faster."

"I know, I know," Lap said with concern. "But too much of a good thing can sometimes be a bad thing. A young boy should be out with girls, having fun. Seeing some movies or going to the mall."

"That will come later," Johnny explained. "I've got a lot of work to do."

Lap smiled and nodded. He understood where Johnny's mind-set was. He added, "You know Johnny Powers, I can help you improve your strength. No problem. I can guarantee it."

This perked up Johnny's interests. He asked, "How's that?"

Lap waved him on to follow. He took Johnny's shoulder and pointed him to the loading dock. He said, "Easily! You do some strength training. The delivery is here. You can put it in the cooler."

Johnny just chuckled and made for the loading dock. Dan, the delivery driver leaned against back of the truck waiting for Johnny to unloaded the store's order.

"Hey Johnny," he said. "Did you see it last night? The Warrior Fights?"

Johnny shook his head. He replied, "I didn't, I wasn't home. Were they intense?"

"Dude, they were EPIC! One of the Warriors got in the ring with some unknown gang fighter and they went the full five minutes. Just when you thought the new kid was going to actually do it, the Warrior knocked him solid into next week. BAM! Out cold."

Johnny stopped to listen to the story and he looked up into the distance, daydreaming about what it must have been like.

"Wow," Johnny said. "Out cold?"

Dan just nodded.

Lap came out the back door and grabbed a crate of lettuce from the cooler on the truck. He looked at the two dreamers staring into oblivion and grabbed their attention.

"Blah, blah, blah. Everybody wants to fight, nobody wants

to load the cooler."

He turned back into the store to put the lettuce away. Johnny and Dan look at each other with a laugh and grabbed boxes to bring inside.

In the cooler, Dan continued his conversation about the W.F.C..

"Every fighter and gang member in town is trying out for that show. They say you get paid even if you just get tossed around. Have you thought about trying out? You're totally good enough to get some attention."

"I never really put that much mind to it. I mean, I read about the try-outs, but it's just a TV show, right?"

"I don't know." Dan shrugged. "The guys who they pit up against the Warriors are real guys from gangs in Metropolis. Some guys are supposed to be top ranked amateurs and even they don't have your moves."

"I don't know Dan. I probably need more practice."

Dan shrugged and said, "Well, if you do try, at least you can say you gave it a shot."

Johnny nodded in agreement. Just then Lap walked into the cooler with the last box from the deliver truck.

"You want practice? I kick you in the behind if you don't stop daydreaming."

Dan jumped back with a big "HA!"

"Okay, good day. You come back tomorrow," Lap said, scooting Dan out the cooler door.

Dan left laughing with Lap waving him off on his way. Lap then turned toward Johnny. He started to make slow swinging motions at Johnny. Johnny chuckled and ducked, spinning away slowly.

"I'm not bad for an old man, hmmm?" Lap said.

They could barely control their laughter.

"Not bad Mr. Huon.," Johnny said, dodging and deflecting the slow motion shots Lap took at him. "Not bad at all."

Chapter 3

When Johnny arrived home from work, his mother Maria was waiting at the kitchen table.

"You weren't here for breakfast again. Did you go to work early?" she asked.

"I left early to get a workout in Mom."

This got Maria flustered.

"Is that all you think about anymore Johnny? Karate fighting and working out? Early mornings, late nights! No social life?"

Johnny rolled his eyes and raised his voice. He had heard this complaint over and over and he was getting tired of hearing it.

"What friends Mom?" he argued. "My classmates went off to college last year. I work and I work out. That IS my social life!"

Maria realized that she was fighting an up hill battle, but as his mother, she felt it was her duty to fuel this fire.

"You concentrate so much on fighting. I have to wonder if it's really that healthy. I read a column in woman's Weekly about teenage relationships …"

Johnny interrupted.

"Enough Mom, please. I talked to Dan at work today and he's got me set on an idea. I want to compete on the Warrior Fights, that's where the best fighters are!"

Maria was aghast.

"Best Fighters?" she barked. "Oooh, you're just like your father! All he wanted was to be the best. Always training, always in the gym."

"And what's wrong with that? Dad trained every day and some said he WAS the best. He earned a Medal of Honor! You don't just get one of those for attendance!"

Maria turned toward the mantle where a picture of her late husband showed him wearing a military uniform. In a small glass box, in front of the picture, was his Medal of Honor. She exhaled with a deep sigh.

"When he was in the hospital he told me that he wished

he'd spent more time with his family. I wish you'd think the same way. I don't want you to have that kind of regret."

Dan defended his father and said, "Dad spent plenty of time with me."

Maria turned back to Johnny with empathy this time. She was well aware that this was Johnny's life. It was in his DNA to feel so strongly.

"Always fighting though, all that time you spent together was spent training in your Tae Kwon Do."

Johnny pleaded a last time. He said calmly, "He just wanted me to achieve the best of what I could be!"

"It's not bad to meet your potential Johnny, I just don't want you to miss out on any chances in life. If you're always in the gym, you might miss them."

Johnny rolled his eyes again, but the air lightened in the room. He knew she just wanted him to be happy and to have every opportunity in life. He gave her a hug for reassurance.

"I'll be okay mom, don't worry," he said.

As she hugged him, Johnny looked at the picture of his father and the medal on the mantle. It represented everything he worked for. Honor and dedication.

Maria changed her tone. She moved toward the refrigerator and asked, "Can I fix you some dinner?"

Johnny thought about it and grabbed his jacket off the back of a kitchen chair.

"You know what Mom?" he said, standing tall with a smirky smile. "I'm going to go out. I'll grab a pizza."

Maria was happy at this response. She thought that maybe she was reaching him after all.

"Well, get home early," she called behind him. "Top athletes need a good night's sleep."

Johnny had to laugh inside. He knew she had his best interests at heart. He called back, "Now Mom, I'm going out after all. I'll sleep in tomorrow morning, okay?"

"Hey," she remarked. "You're still my baby boy – don't you forget it!" She waved from inside the house and said, "You just go have a nice time."

Johnny headed out, leaving Maria smiling as she closed the door behind him.

Chapter 4

Johnny was driving his pick-up truck home with his pizza. The streets looked cold and hard, peppered by neon signs on storefronts that hadn't been boarded up yet. Most had some sort of chain-link protection over the windows and doors. It seemed a shame that this is what downtown Metropolis had become.

The smell of the pizza was tempting Johnny to take a slice. He pulled up to a yellow light and instead of running through it, he decided it was the perfect place to stop and grab a slice. As he looked over at the pie on the passenger seat something unusual drew his attention to an empty office building parking lot. It looked like three Latin hoodlums harassing a lone Chinese girl. He suddenly forgot about the pizza.

He pulled his truck into the empty parking lot and turned the wheel toward the four bodies in the lot. He dropped the transmission into park and jumped out the door. The three thugs turned to this potential threat. Preparing for what may come, one of the gang members grabbed the girl from behind by her shoulders.

The thug who appeared to be the leader of the group called out asking, "What brings you here Vato? Ain't you got nothing better to do with your time?"

Johnny was as quick with his words as he was on his feet. He reached into the truck and grabbed the pizza box from the seat.

"Pizza delivery service!" he replied.

The hooligan voiced back. "You got the wrong address dude! Nobody here ordered no Goddamned pizza, did we guys?"

They all laughed amongst themselves and their tone turned a little more rowdy. The girl squeaked out a single word.

~ Help!~

The dirt-bag holding her back put his fingerless glove over her mouth and pulled her close to him.

Johnny met her stare eye to eye and gave her a silent assurance that in just a minute, she'd be fine.

The leader piped back up. "I said we ordered no pizzas man! Why are you still here?!"

Johnny approached them with a few steps and they inched back, just a bit. Control was in Johnny's favor.

"Are you sure?" he asked, opening the box and revealing a warm and toasty double cheese with extra sauce. "I was told to deliver this amazing pie to the three idiots in the parking lot at Fifth and Main."

The gang members all looked hungrily at the pizza. Their laugh turned from threatening to greedy.

One of the second hand thugs voiced up. "Hey boss, this hero thinks were idiots."

The leader laughed again. "Why don't you just give it to us and get the hell out of here before we kick your ass!"

"Okay", Johnny said and he launched the hot slices at the gang leader. Leaping forward, he delivered a series of kicks and punches into the head, chest and stomach of the mouthy second hand hoodlum.

Looking down at the pizza that now decorated the front of his shirt, the leader yelled, "Get him!"

The punk that held the girl let her go and she ran a few steps away and stopped to witness the carnage.

Now without the girl in his hands, the thug took a shot at

Johnny. When he stepped in, Johnny close-lined him and his dirty shoes went flying up over his head. He dropped flat onto his back with a thud. Johnny followed up with a high kick to the face of the other second hand thug who had just got to his feet. He stood to face the leader.

The leader pulled off his pizza covered shirt and revealed a thin and muscular frame covered with gang tattoos. He flexed his arms in a small territorial display of power and stood back in a ready stance.

"Bring it punk!" he yelled to Johnny.

Johnny had a grin that ran ear to ear. This was like a dream come true. Live targets! He bounced on his toes and made a Bruce Lee type of taunt at the hoodlum.

"Huuaaaahhh."

The hoodlum stepped in and Johnny kicked out at his side and found his kick caught by the krafty thug. He had some experience, but so did Johnny. Johnny backhanded his opponents cheek and followed through with three quick punches to the middle of his face before his body dropped to the parking lot.

Johnny three, gang trash zero!

The girl came up next to Johnny and looked down at the three pieces of trash that had harassed her now lying out cold on the pavement. Johnny turned his smile over his shoulder and spoke.

"Was that okay?"

The girl look up at him, she was a good few inches shorter. She nodded repeatedly with a smile.

"Um, hmm!"

"Are you hurt?"

She shook her head side to side. "Mmm,mmm."

"Do you talk?" Johnny asked smiling really wide.

"Hi. I'm May Ling. Thank you for coming to my rescue. That was truly unexpected."

Johnny was a little confused at the entire situation. A girl alone on the streets of Metropolis at night? She obviously wasn't aware of the obvious danger that was involved.

"Why are you out here alone at night? It's not safe for a girl to be on the streets alone," he stated. "This city is one gang after another."

She shrugged. "I was waiting for a Taxi. I worked late in those offices over there. They said they would be here fifteen minutes ago."

Johnny looked around. No taxi, no cars, no people. It was clear and obvious that the taxi wouldn't be arriving any time soon.

"I don't think they're coming," he said.

May looked around and she had to agree. She sighed.

"Can I offer you a ride home?" Johnny asked.

May smiled and took Johnny's hand with both of her hands. She looked longingly up at him and said, "That would be a great help. How can I refuse?"

Johnny stepped over a hoodlum and around to the passenger side of his pick-up truck. He opened the door and May Ling climbed into the cab. The smell the pie that was now spread across the parking lot wafted out the door of the cab. They both took a whiff.

Johnny said, "I'd offer you a slice of pizza, but …"

They laughed and Johnny shut her door. He ran around to the driver's side and hopped in. A turn of the key and they headed out to the street.

As they drove, May Ling pointed out directions to her home. She told Johnny how she came out for the Taxi but wasn't able to get back inside when she saw the thugs.

She was helpless and he was her hero.

"When we get home," she said, "I would like you to come in and meet my grandfather. He will be grateful to hear what you've done."

"You live with your grandfather?" Johnny replied.

"Yes. My parents live in China. My grandfather moved here when I was a little girl, and after high school I came to America to live with him."

"Ahh," Johnny said, raising a finger. "The land of golden opportunities?"

May Ling smiled and looked out at the depressed streets and closed storefronts they passed.

"So it would seem," she said.

Arriving at her house, Johnny pulled the truck up the driveway. They were met by Grandfather at the door. He was clearly upset.

"Look what the cat brought in!" Grandfather said sternly.

"Grandfather," May offered. "This gentleman came to my rescue tonight."

Grandfather flailed his arms in the air.

"This I know. It's all over the television. They see you, and him," he pointed at Johnny. "They caught your license plate and even the news man knows your name now Mr. Johnny Powers, vigilante hero!"

Grandfather turned to scold May.

"You should know better than to be outside alone at night. It's not where you belong!"

May bowed her head down and replied, "I know better now Grandfather."

Grandfather turned back to Johnny and the lecture continued.

"And you! Are you so stupid that you would try to get yourself killed for the likes of my granddaughter? Hmmm?"

He leaned in close to Johnny, staring him dead in the face.

Johnny was taken by surprise at the line of questioning but he kept a respectful cool.

"Yes sir, I do believe I would."

"So tough that three men who might be armed with

knives or even guns don't scare you? Hmmm?"

Johnny replied, "I was only concerned with May's safety."

Grandfather stepped back. He looked Johnny up and down and relaxed his pose.

"Well then, I thank you for protecting the life of my granddaughter. I am in your debt."

May Ling hugged her grandfather with a big smile on her face. He accepted the affection like an old scrooge and waved her off.

"Now-now, enough of that," he said. "Come inside and offer our guest some tea."

With the warmer reception, they followed Grandfather into the house.

While sitting around a coffee table and sipping tea, Grandfather told the story of what he saw on television.

"… and as I am watching the news, I see you fighting with those hooligans, and May Ling is there. The security camera saw everything. Just after you left the police arrived and arrested those boys."

"I hope they get punished for what they have done." May Ling said. "They should go away for a long time!"

"If justice serves true, they will be punished," Grandfather replied. "Enough of this newscast. Johnny, tell me, who is your teacher?"

Johnny welcomed any opportunity to talk about his training. Nothing thrilled him more.

"I learned from my father," he boasted. "As long as I can remember, he was training me to be my best."

"And he trains you today then?" Grandfather asked.

Johnny looked down toward the floor. He sadly shook his head slightly from side to side.

"No. My father passed away about four years ago from cancer."

Grandfather offered a few seconds of silence before responding.

"I offer my sympathies."

"Thank you Grandfather. He was a great man."

Grandfather offered kind words to soften the moment. He told Johnny, "I can see this. It is evident in your actions."

Grandfather finished his tea with a final gulp.

"Is your mother at home then?"

Johnny perked up, realizing that she may be wondering where he is.

"Yes, she is," Johnny said.

"It is possible then that she has seen this too. You should call her to ease any concerns," Grandfather suggested.

Johnny stood to his feet.

"She worries a lot!" he said. "I wasn't thinking that she might be watching the news. I should get right home."

As Johnny made ready for his goodbyes Grandfather and May Ling joined him.

"Can I see you again Johnny Powers?" May asked.

"I work all day tomorrow at Huon's General Store on Main Street. If you want to call me there, we could make some plans."

"I know just where that is. I will call you," May said happily.

Grandfather interjected.

"I know Lap Huon well. He is a good man and a good friend. May I ask how you come to know him?"

Johnny explained saying, "He served with my father in the military and has been very good to me since my father passed away. He gave me a job when I turned fifteen and he lets me practice in the back of his store."

Grandfather nodded knowing that if his friend trusts Johnny, he too can have faith in Johnny's character.

"Please. Before you go, I would like to show you one thing," Grandfather requested.

Johnny was a little puzzled, but was always receptive to criticism.

"When that gang member caught your kick, you might have tried something more effective."

He motioned for Johnny to stand in the open area away from the furniture.

"You be the hooligan," he instructed.

Grandfather threw a kick like a young teenaged boy. Johnny raised both arms up and caught it at his side, holding it like the gang member did to him.

With superior balance, Grandfather did not retreat and

regroup. He held the pose, motioning with his head for Johnny to look down.

When Johnny looked down, he saw that grandfather had a fist just centimeters from Johnny's groin. Johnny let go of Grandfather's leg.

"That is another option for you to consider," Grandfather noted. "Should you get caught again."

Johnny bowed slightly with gratitude.

"Thank you Grandfather. I will practice it regularly."

Grandfather nodded, bidding Johnny farewell before he turned and left the two teenagers to say goodbye.

"Thank you for coming in for tea," May said.

"Thank YOU. I've never met anyone quite like your Grandfather. He really surprised me."

"He holds a lot of knowledge. He is truly a great man," May said warmly. She loved her grandfather dearly.

"I would have to agree," Johnny replied.

May leaned in and reached her arms around Johnny's back. She gave him an awkward and unexpected hug. Johnny welcomed the affection and hugged back.

"I'll talk to you tomorrow then?" Johnny asked.

May Ling smiled. "Yes," she said. "Tomorrow."

Johnny stepped out the door to get home quickly with May Ling watching him climb into his truck. She was smitten.

Maria was waiting by the door when Johnny came in. She rushed to him and threw her arms around her son.

"I saw you on the news," she said frantically. "I was so worried about you. I'm sorry I told you to go out for the night. I'm sorry Johnny."

She held him tightly.

"I'm okay Mom. Really."

Johnny made some space between them and took off his jacket.

"Those boys are going to jail. The news reporter said that you're a hero now. "

Johnny grinned demurely. He said, "I'm no hero Mom. I did what anyone would have done."

Maria was elated. She boasted, "My boy, a celebrity. I

can't wait to tell all the girls when I get my hair done."

Johnny put his jacket over the back of a chair and made for the stairs.

Maria called behind him. "The news people were here, they asked to talk to you. They wanted to wait outside for you to get home but I chased them off. "

"Thanks Mom," Johnny said. "I'm going to bed now, I'm tired."

Johnny headed upstairs to his bedroom.

"You rest up now," Maria told him. She whispered to herself with pride, "My son the hero. Who would have known?"

Chapter 5

When Johnny got to work there were news vans from Channel Four, Five and Seven parked on the street in front of the store. They were waiting to spring on him with a barrage of interview questions.

Johnny parked down the block and from the moment he stepped out of his truck the reporters were right in his face. It was all he could do to get through them and into the store. Once inside, Lap came storming down an aisle, frustrated to no end.

"They have been here for an hour already!" Lap hollered. "They won't leave until you talk to them. Please, make them go away, we have a business to run!"

Johnny walked toward the back room followed by news cameras and reporters. The filed in behind him, filling the spaces between the five rows of shelves in the small store. Each of the reporters fought for a chance to ask Johnny their burning questions.

Channel Five asked first, "Johnny, can you tell us what

happened last night, in your own words?"

"Yeah," Johnny replied, "I saw three guys giving a girl a hard time and I went to see if she needed help."

Channel Seven asked, "Did you know this girl personally before last night?"

"No, I didn't."

Channel Four asked, "Is this a warning to the gang members in Metropolis that we the people will not stand for harassment anymore?"

This question struck a chord with Johnny.

"I can't speak for anyone else, but I will say that I don't think it's fair for any guys to beat up on a defenseless girl. That's just wrong!"

Channel Four jumped back in asking, "Can you tell us about your martial arts training?"

"What do you want to know?"

"How long have you been in training?"

"All my life," Johnny said with pride.

"And do you train in these facilities?"

Off to the side, Lap shook his head, NO, NO, NO!

Johnny shut the back room door and responded insisting, "That's privileged information."

Finally, Channel Five asked the question that viewers would be sure to want to an answer to.

"Johnny, will we get the chance to see you compete on Channel Five's Warrior Fights?"

There was a long moment of silence as everyone leaned in with their microphones, eager to hear his response.

"I don't know," Johnny said.

Lap jumped in between Johnny and the reporters waving is hands. He shouted, "I have a business to run here! You can go now! No more questions!"

The news crews disbanded with Lap is chasing them all the way out. The Channel Seven Camera Guy passed a word on to Johnny as he left.

"I hope you're around when my daughter needs help. Good job son."

Johnny responded warmly. He was glad someone finally took the commercial edge off of it and simply said thank you.

"I'll do my best," Johnny said with a smile.

They shook hands and the reporter crews filed out.

Back at the W.F.C., Gary was seated at his desk when the league's Champion Fighter came bursting through the door. He was known as The Punisher. He was flanked by two of the suit and tie Warrior Fight's personnel, Tim Watts and Fred Delaney.

Gary looked up from his paperwork to see an angry Punisher staring down at him. Close to six and a half feet tall and built like a steam locomotive, he started barking through his black and white W.F.C. mask at Gary. Gary didn't flinch.

"Here's how it is man! The Punisher wants more coverage, more fame and more money! Especially more money!"

Gary leaned back in his chair. It was always about money with these guys.

"Punisher, babe," Gary conned him in a soothing tone. "What more can I give you? You're already The Warrior Fights Champion. "

The Punisher was definitely not satisfied.

Gary pointed to a chair and asked, "Would you like to have a seat and talk about this?"

The Punisher tossed the chair to the side. He continued his ranting, "The Punisher doesn't want to sit or talk. I want to see the numbers in my bank account getting bigger. For Christ's sake, I only made a two hundred thousand dollars last year. "

Gary motioned for Fred to close the door. In a calm and rational tone, he tried to subdue The Punisher with words.

"You know all about the opportunities we arrange for eager fighters," Gary shared. "Those can benefit you as well as anyone else in the company who can keep it quiet. You know what you have to do."

The Punisher stood tall. He was as insulted as he was insulting.

"Your fixed matches? I know all about those set ups. So what! You don't have anyone here who's going to beat The Punisher, and The Punisher doesn't throw matches for anyone. I am, and will remain, The W.F.C. Champion."

Gary responded, "Fist threw a match and made ten thousand dollars. You could call that good money for a night's work, eh?"

The Punisher had enough of this. He belted out a final warning yelling, "The Punisher ain't going to blow his title for one of your petty set-ups. I can beat anyone you've got! Consider that when you make your bets. The Punisher always wins his matches! Always!"

The Punisher stormed out of the office in a huff. Gary looked up at Tim and Fred as they watched him go.

"And that, my friends," Gary said, "is why I always take the bets against him. I'd say it's worked out well so far."

They all laughed in agreement. Their goal was getting rich off the sweat of someone else, and they were doing that quite well.

Tim picked up the fallen chair and the three sat to talk.

Gary asked, "What do you guys think? Is he too much?"

Tim shook his head disapprovingly and offered a thought stating, "He's a real poor sport."

Fred agreed. He nodded in agreement and added, "A bad image for the team."

"But you know what?" Gary remarked. "He makes us a whole lot of money."

"How long can that last? People will eventually grow

tired of his antics and his attitude," Fred said.

Tim added, "Warrior Fights needs a new face. Someone the people can fall in love with."

Peter Thorn, the Press relations Representative for the W.F.C. came through the door excitedly.

"You guys have GOT to see this," he said, calling their attention to a DVD he had in his hand. He proceeded to press open on the DVD player in the corner of the office, sparking the TV to life.

Gary reached over and pulled down a window shade. He asked, "What have you got there?"

"This kid was all over the news last night. They're calling him a hero! Today he got on camera and one of our boys was there."

The news reel came up on the TV screen. The four men were locked in on every word.

They heard the voice of the Channel Four Reporter ask, "And do you train in these facilities?"

Johnny's reply came over video footage of the back room that was captured through the open door at Huon's before Johnny shut it.

"That's privileged information."

Peter pointed to the screen. Inserted footage showed the room with five sandbags hanging in various places.

"Look at this place," he said with awe. "Bags hanging everywhere? Our guys don't train like that! Does this kid think he's Sylvester Stallone or something!"

The voice of their own Channel Five Reporter came on next.

"Johnny, will we ever get the chance to see you compete on Channel Five's Warrior Fights?"

Gary pointed at the screen with a smile. He let out, "That man deserves a pay raise."

The voice of Johnny responded from the DVD saying, "I don't know."

Peter stopped the recording. He added, "This kid took out three street gang members last night for harassing a girl he didn't even know. One of them was a winner in one of our fights three months ago!"

Tim asked, "Can we get him?"

Gary took control of where the conversation was going.

"It's not a matter of can we, it's when do we? Somebody get me this kid's number. We have to let him know we want to see him fight. No, that we expect to see him fight!"

"Right away," Peter said as he jumped up and left the office.

"Boys, I'm willing to bet that for the right price, we just found our new Golden Child," Gary said.

Fred and Tim nodded and smiled in agreement.

Chapter 6

Grandfather reviewed the news footage of the ordeal again. As he watched he nodded, impressed at Johnny's abilities. When the newsreel ended a commercial for Warrior Fights came on. Grandfather raised his hands and waved them at the screen in disgust.

"Warriors," he exclaimed out loud. "Bah! That's child's play."

At work, Johnny picked up the ringing telephone saying, "Huon's General Store."

The caller answered, "I'd like to speak with Johnny Power please."

"It's Johnny Powers," Johnny corrected. "with an 'S' … and you have him."

"Hi Johnny. This is Gary Grasier, producer of Warrior Fights on Channel Five, maybe you've heard of us."

"Of course I have!" Johnny said, surprised at the call.

"Of course you have, who am I fooling? We're ranked in primetime's top five. Johnny, I'll cut right to the chase here, no holds barred."

"Just like your matches?" Johnny interjected.

"I like that Johnny," Gary chuckled. "You've got wit, but let me get to the point. We saw you on television and we would like it if you would come down to our gym and get in the ring with a couple of fighters from our program. "

Johnny was taken by surprise and didn't offer any response as Gary continued his appeal.

"How would you feel about that Johnny? I can call you Johnny, can't I?"

"You can call me Johnny if you want to, but I'm not sure I'd be any match for a Warrior Fighter, Mister Grasier."

"Don't underestimate yourself kid, and call me Gary, please. Besides, we can give you a couple of amateurs just to see you move. After all, that's what we're looking to do. We just want to see your abilities. See some of that star material shine."

Johnny's excitement built. He did his best to play it cool as Dan walked in from the loading dock to make the daily delivery. Johnny waved him over, making a hushing gesture with his finger over his lips.

"I think I can do that," Johnny said into the phone.

"Fantastic," Gary replied. "Do you know where the arena is?"

"I sure do!"

"Why don't you come down tomorrow morning, say, eleven o'clock?"

"I'll be there. Eleven o'clock," Johnny confirmed.

"Great," Gary said, satisfied in the response. "And Johnny, bring some of that star potential."

When they hung up Johnny turned to Dan. He was leaning on the counter focusing his full attention on Johnny's call.

"What is it?" Dan asked. Just by seeing Johnny's excitement on the phone he was sure this had to be good news of some sort.

"It's the Warrior fights." Johnny burst out. "They want me to try out! Like how you were telling me!"

"Alright! It's about time!" Dan said giving Johnny a high five.

The phone rang again as Johnny made his first step toward the delivery. He turned back to answer it wondering how life could possibly be better.

"Let me get this, I'll be back there in a minute," he said to Dan.

Dan made for the loading dock and Johnny answered the phone.

"Huon's General Store," he said, as he always did.

"Johnny?" the little voice squeaked. It was May Ling, calling as promised.

"May Ling, Hi."

"Johnny, my Grandfather and I would be happy to have you over for dinner this evening. Would you join us?"

"I can't wait," Johnny answered blissfully. "I have some great news to share."

"Then I look forward to it. Dinner is at five-thirty," May responded.

"I'll see you then. Bye."

Lap came up to Johnny as he hung up the telephone. He

asked, "Good news on the phone?"

"More than you know Mr. Huon." Johnny boasted. "Things are looking up."

"Good-good," Lap said as he scooted Johnny toward the loading dock. "Now go get my tomatoes."

Chapter 7

Grandfather was milling around the living room, making an open space in the middle of the room. May Ling was preparing the kitchen table for their guest. She came into the living room to see what Grandfather was up to.

"Grandfather, what are you doing?" she asked.

"Nothing to concern you. Pay me no mind."

May smiled and asked, "But why are you moving the furniture?"

"You have trust in your Grandfather and let me do what it is I do. I know what I am doing with the furniture."

May's attention was caught by the lights of Johnny's truck pulling into the driveway. Grandfather pointed out the fact and said, "Your guest has arrived."

He picked up a small antique clock from the center of the end table.

"And right on time too," he said while putting the clock up on the fireplace mantle, seemingly out of the way.

May Ling scampered to the door. Grandfather smugly called after her, "Don't seem so excited dear, he might think you like him."

May opened the door and met Johnny at the top stair. They shared a long gaze, happy to see one another. Johnny pulled a small bouquet of flowers from behind his back and handed them to May. She blushed.

"Hello May Ling," he said warmly.

She got up on her tippy-toes and kissed him on the cheek.

"Come in Johnny, please."

Walking through the door, Grandfather came to meet with them.

"Hello Grandfather," Johnny said. "I have something for you too"

Johnny produced a small wooden box in his other hand. The outside of the box was covered with Chinese writing. Grandfather took it with a smile and looked it over.

"It's green leaf tea from China," Johnny said.

Grandfather smiled and replied gratefully, "It is my favorite of all Chinese tea. Thank you."

Grandfather gestured to come into the house. Dinner was ready to enjoy together.

During the course of eating Johnny shared the events of the day.

"So I answered the telephone," he explained. "It was the head of Warrior Fighting. He said he saw me on TV and would like me to try out for the show."

May was delighted. She perked up and asked, "You will be on television again?"

"I might, and maybe I'll get to fight with the Warriors."

Grandfather broke into Johnny's excitement. He was less than impressed at the opportunity.

"That's not real fighting," he said.

Johnny rebutted, "It looks real to me."

Grandfather grew instantly irritated. He said back sternly, "And what do you know of real fighting?"

May jumped in, begging Grandfather to be kind. She

pleaded, "Grandfather, please. He wants to try."

"Learning the art of fighting takes a long time Johnny Powers, many years of practice," Grandfather pointed out.

Johnny was on the defensive, knowing well he worked hard to get where he was in his training. While for many years now he had trained alone, it had been rigorous none-the-less.

"I've been practicing all of my life," Johnny argued.

Grandfather fired back. He hoped to reach Johnny's common sense.

"I have also been practicing all of your life. And," Grandfather added, "all of my life too."

"But these people are tough," Johnny pointed out. "Real angry and real mean."

"Is it anger that makes a person tough? Makes them mean?" Grandfather asked, continuing to verbally slap Johnny down at his every remark.

May Ling looked terribly upset. She begged, "Grandfather, you said you wouldn't."

"With all due respect sir, these people are Warriors!" Johnny stated.

"Poppycock!" Grandfather burst out. "These are no warriors. They have no dignity, no pride in their art or it's heritage! They are street fighters and screen actors! No different than the thugs who assaulted May Ling!"

Johnny had no response. Grandfather continued to try to teach Johnny a lesson.

"Do I look angry to you?" Grandfather asked.

"No."

"A mean person am I?"

"I don't think so," Johnny replied.

Grandfather stood from the table. He summoned Johnny to join him in the area he previously cleared furniture from.

"Show me what these warriors call fighting," Grandfather commanded. Johnny was befuddled.

"You want me to fight you?" he asked Grandfather.

Grandfather burst out in laughter at Johnny's question. He poked back saying, "You fight me? Ha ha! Give me your best shot hero."

Johnny moved a kick at Grandfather, but with little force or aggression. Grandfather pushed it back at him.

"This is how you fought to protect my Granddaughter? This is the fighter that made the six-o-clock news? You will have to do better than that to beat up on these so called warriors."

Johnny was still perplexed. He said, "I don't want to…"

"What?" Grandfather barked. "Hurt an old man?"

"Well, yeah."

This brought a very wide smile and belittling laugh to Grandfather. He couldn't hold back the chuckles.

"If you could hurt me Johnny Powers," Grandfather said, "I would move back to China this instant and become a monk. Now you attack me as if your life depended on it."

Johnny stepped back and hesitated for a moment. He nodded to Grandfather as if to see that he was ready.

"Don't you worry about this old man, you just worry about yourself!" Grandfather said with a little laugh.

May Ling stood in the kitchen doorway and shook her head side to side. She put her forehead in her hand because she knew what was about to happen.

Johnny stepped forward and made a simultaneous kick and punch combination. Grandfather twisted Johnny's body over in mid air. He landed flat on the floor with a bruised ego.

Grandfather stood over him. Johnny looked up at May Ling and she just shrugged as if she too was unsuspecting of what had just transpired. The truth is, she knew what was going on.

"Again," Grandfather commanded. "This time you try!"

Johnny regrouped. He tried a different strategy. A spinning kick, as if he would impress Grandfather with some acrobatics. Grandfather swatted him down from the air like a common housefly.

Johnny looked up at Grandfather in disbelief. Grandfather just nodded his head at the failure. Several more attempts resulted in the same end until Grandfather thought Johnny had learned enough of this lesson.

May Ling came in to the living room with a tray of tea and cookies. Now that things had settled, dessert was in order.

Johnny sat and pleaded with Grandfather.

"I could learn so much from you. I didn't realize. Would

you teach me how to fight like a true warrior?"

"What you have learned here is lesson enough," Grandfather replied. "Take that knowledge and use it in your own studies."

"But in my own studies I am alone," Johnny answered.

"Just as you were when you came to my granddaughter's rescue. What now do you need of a teacher?"

This was more than an uphill battle for Johnny, Grandfather was immoveable on the subject.

"With you, I could be the best that I can be."

"Tomorrow you fight just like this. If you give your best, then that is the best you can be. That is all there is to learn."

Forgetting the hope of a new teacher, Johnny hung his head and accepted the reality with understanding.

"I understand Grandfather," he spoke. "Thank you for all you have shown me tonight."

Grandfather stood and bowed a little toward Johnny and left the room.

May Ling came to Johnny's side to comfort him. She knew

his hopes and she was sympathetic to his being disheartened.

"He can seem to be a strange old man, but he means well," she assured him. "He knows best."

"He has a lot of knowledge. If he could teach me more … wow. Since my father's passing I have dreamt of a teacher who could make me shine. Your Grandfather could be that person."

"You will be great tomorrow. Even Grandfather thinks it, he said so."

"You're right," Johnny sighed. "I will do my best."

Johnny took May's hand.

"I should go. I'll be working at Huon's after the try-out if you want to know how I did. I can call you."

"I do not work tomorrow. I will come to the store so you can tell me how you performed."

"You will?" Johnny asked happily.

May Ling smiled and nodded affirmatively.

"Of course Johnny. I believe in you."

In Johnny's mind, nothing else mattered at that moment. He was falling in love.

May Ling leaned in and kissed Johnny quickly. It was so unexpected that it made him red in the cheeks.

"For Luck," May said.

Johnny smiled and simply replied, "Thank you."

As Johnny pulled out of the drive, May Ling closed the door and leaned back against the kitchen wall drifting into La-La Land. She was in love.

From the other room Grandfather looked on, smiling at what had transpired.

Chapter 8

The daily events at the Warrior Fights Arena included fighters coming in and out of the gym to exercise, electricians working on camera equipment and lighting and office personnel doing what ever it was they did.

Johnny entered the arena with a bag over his shoulder. There were fighters sparring and stretching all over the arena floor. Gary was talking with a fighter when Johnny came into view. He broke away to greet him.

"Johnny Power! I recognize that face from TV."

"Hi," Johnny said, not sure who Gary was.

"It's Gary. Gary Grasier. We spoke on the telephone?"

"There are a lot of people here," Johnny mentioned. "I thought it was just a try out?"

"Well Johnny, as you can imagine, every fighter in Metropolis wants a shot on Warrior Fights. These ARE the try-outs."

Johnny looked over the room. There were literally two
dozen fighters in all sorts of outfits working out in the
arena. It was easy to spot the stars of the show by their
elaborate and colorful outfits. Still, all around the room
were street fighters, gang members and thugs that
looked to score their fifteen minutes of fame on prime
time TV.

"Is there a place I can change up?" Johnny asked.

Gary pointed to the locker rooms.

"Right through those doors. Take your time and warm up.
I'll see you out here when you're ready. We'll be pairing
up fighters for the try-outs."

"Cool," Johnny replied as he headed for the locker room.

He turned back to Gary and said, "One other thing. It's
Powers … with an S."

Gary's fake TV smile faded fast as Johnny left the arena
floor. Sheila came to his side.

"Is that him? The TV hero?" she asked.

"So they say," Gary answered. He waved for Warrior
Fighters Blade and Gunner to come over to him.

"He doesn't look so tough," Sheila said. "Hmmph."

Gary grabbed Blade's shoulder and laid out a plan.

"Blade, let a couple of the unknowns have their way the Powers kid so we can see what he's made of. If he lives through that, I want Gunner to give him a shot."

Blade acknowledged the plan. "Yes Mister Grasier."

"We'll be upstairs watching."

Gunner and Blade nodded and headed off to do their duty.

Johnny came out of the locker room in a white Tae Kwon Do uniform with a black belt. Sheila nodded her head in Johnny's direction.

"Introduce me to the Golden Boy," she said.

Gary called to Johnny. He came trotting over, bouncing on his toes to warm up a bit.

"Johnny, this is my partner Sheila. She wanted an opportunity to meet you."

"Hello," Johnny greeted her, extending a taped up right hand. Sheila looked him up and down, biting her lip as she did. It was an obvious sizing up.

"A black belt, eh?"

"Yeah. I got this when I was twelve but it still fits, so I wear it on my practice uniform."

Sheila feigned being impressed.

Gary directed Johnny's attention to Blade, at ringside.

"Johnny, that's Blade over there. He's one of our Warriors and he's going to fix you up with some matches. We'll be upstairs watching you shine."

Johnny nodded in understanding and made his way over to Blade. Gary signaled to Blade, 'two minutes'. Blade nodded in affirmation.

In the upstairs office there were five men, Asian business types, in blue suits. They sat at a table in the window that overlooks the arena. Gary and Sheila came into the office.

"Gentlemen. What you have here is the first chance to see and judge who may become our next big investment."

The men all turned to look down on the ring. Johnny was climbing into it.

One of the business men perked up and said, "Oh, news

boy Johnny Powers."

The rest of the men leaned over for a better view and they chattered among themselves.

Gary and Sheila took up a spot on the other side of the room.

"I hope your Golden Boy makes the grade Gary."

"It doesn't much matter. We can make him look like a superstar against anyone. He just needs the right moves."

They chuckled deviously between themselves.

Everyone in the gym was eager to see Johnny's performance. Activities came to a halt and everyone turned to get a look at the ring. On the far side of the gym, nearly unseen, The Punisher looked on from a back room doorway. He wasn't all too happy to see Johnny getting that kind of attention.

Johnny got into his corner, bouncing in his steps. Spider, a typical street type gang member who was also trying out for the show climbed through the ropes.

Spider walked toward Johnny and taunted him.

"So I get to take apart the TV star who doesn't like the gangs in Metropolis?"

Johnny didn't respond to the remark. Spider seated a fist into his other hand, continuing to taunt.

Blade came into the ring. He was to referee the match.

"Okay guys, show us what you've got."

The two fighters circled each other. Spider led in with an attack and Johnny blocked all the hits. Spider slipped one through and tagged Johnny on the side of the face. They each stepped back to regroup.

"This ain't TV news punk. You got the master to stand up to, so bring it on!" the hooligan shouted.

Johnny wiped his lip where a small amount of blood started to form and he put his hands up, setting himself into a fighting position.

Spider led in again, but before he raised a hand to strike, Johnny drove straight punch to his nose and splattered him all over the mat. Knocked out cold!

Upstairs, the business men jumped to their feet and gathered in front of the window. Gary and Sheila stared at one another in disbelief. The punch was fast … really fast! A single shot took out a prime contender and they were truly in disbelief.

"That's what I call a punch!" Gary said.

"This kid could be full of surprises. Let see if that was a one time deal. Get him into another match."

Blade looked up at the office window and saw Gary signal him to pit Johnny up against another street fighter. Blade waved in Snake. Snake stepped over Spider as two men dragged his limp body out of the ring.

"Wimp!" Snake said to the unconscious Spider.

He looked Johnny up and down and spouted out, "You'll do, hero."

Snake cracked his knuckles and rolled his shoulders, making a big production out of himself. Blade stepped into the middle of the ring.

"Fighters ready?" Blade called out.

He dropped his hand between them. Upstairs, the business men eagerly watched from the bay window. Gary and Sheila had to stand in the office doorway to get a look.

As Snake and Johnny came at one another, Johnny swept Snake with his leg and dropped him flat on the mat. He then rolled over and back fisted Snake's nose into a bloody mess all over his face.

Johnny jumped to his feet quickly, ready to fight. Snake was in a ball, holding his face. Blade stepped in front of Johnny, concluding yet another match.

The room lit up with clapping. Johnny had obviously made a big impression.

Blade directed Johnny telling him, "You can rest up a bit, we'll do it again in a few minutes."

Upstairs in the office the businessmen were clapping and conferring amongst themselves in their foreign tongue. Gary and Sheila paired off on the other side of the room to talk about what they witnessed.

"This kid is HOT!", Sheila said.

"He can definitely hold his own with the unknowns. If we get him on television while he's still the talk of the town, he's going to boost commercial value. We're talking some big sales!"

Gary could barely hold his excitement or keep his composure. Johnny was a sure meal ticket!

Sheila said, "These amateurs aren't where it's at. He's got to look good against our guys."

Gary went to the doorway and signaled Gunner to come

upstairs. It was time to kick it up a notch.

"You're going to put him with a Warrior now?" Sheila asked.

Gary replied, "Nothing too harsh, just something a little more aggressive."

Gunner came to the office door and Gary pulled him aside.

"Do you suppose you could get in the ring with Johnny now and show him what Warrior Fighting is all about?"

"I can do that Mister Graiser," Gunner said.

"Push him to his limits, but don't hurt him. I think we have a winner with guy."

He patted Gunner on the shoulder and nudged him on his way. As Gunner came down the stairs, The Punisher approached him.

"You're going in with this puke?" The Punisher asked.

"Well, yeah," Gunner said.

The Punisher leaned in threateningly. He had demands and he boldly said, "If you don't put him out, he's going to make things difficult around here. The Punisher doesn't need any new faces stealing the glory."

"Grasier said not to hurt him," Gunner told him.

"Grasier said nothing! Think about your bank account. This kid could be getting your paycheck."

Gunner gave this a second thought.

"What should I do?" he asked.

"Make him sorry he came here today!"

Gunner nodded in agreement and headed off to the ring.

Against another wall of the gym, Johnny was stretching and kicking. Blade called him to the ring.

"This round, you're going to spar with Gunner," he told Johnny. "He's going to show you how we really do it around here."

Johnny asked, "Full contact style?"

Gunner walked to the edge of the ring and met Johnny face to face. He said, "If you can handle the guns, sure."

Johnny smirked and said, "I'll do my best." He climbed into the ring.

Gary and joined the businessmen and urged them all to sit and get a good view.

"Gentlemen, this is where we put the new fighters to the test. A one on one with a real Warrior Fighter. If they can still stand after five minutes, they're worth the investment."

One of the businessmen turned to the group and made a bet out loud.

"I bet five thousand dollars that he doesn't last two minutes," the first business man exclaimed.

"I'll take that and bet and add another five thousand that he can go the whole five minutes. Any takers?" another one of them said.

As the shuffled papers, dollar signs were flashing in Gary's eyes. Sheila smiled with excitement.

"I think they like him," she said.

Gary replied, "I like him too!"

Johnny and Gunner squared off in the ring. They circled one another a couple of times and Johnny came in with a direct type of kick. Gunner tossed him to the side like a rag doll.

"You'll have to do better than that Johnny."

Johnny heard Grandfather's voice in his head saying the same thing. He regained his composure and Gunner came in with a flurry of strikes. Johnny managed to fend off Gunner's blows for the first three or four times, but two big hands planted themselves on Johnny's chest and sent him into the ropes. He sprung off them landed face down on the on the mat.

Gunner turned to Blade and shrugged his shoulders. Upstairs, the men shuffled the money around figuring this fight was over.

Johnny cracked his knuckles and jumped to his feet. Springing through the air, he landed a two kick attack on Gunner. Gunner left his feet and hit the corner of the ring completely stunned.

He returned to the fight and the two exchanged a series of arm blows, neither actually harming the other.

Upstairs the men grew more impressed. They watched the full five minute match as the fighters traded blows and defensive strikes. In the end it was all they could do to figure out who won what money.

When it came to the end, Gunner's competitive demeanor changed to a friendly congratulations.

"You're tough kid."

"Thanks," Johnny said while catching his breath. "I think I need a rest now."

Gunner patted Johnny on the shoulder and said, "Me too kid. Me too."

Blade held the ropes apart for Gunner to leave the ring. As Johnny followed Blade addressed him.

"That was some impressive work Mister Powers. I can only imagine Mr. Grasier is equally as impressed."

Gary and Sheila came down the staircase from the upstairs office. Gunner met them at the bottom of the stairs.

"Good job Johnny!" Gary said, disregarding Gunner as he walked past him toward the ring.

"Looked a little tough in there Gunner," Sheila taunted at Gunner as she followed Gary.

Off to one side of the gym, Gunner met with The Punisher.

"What the hell was that about? He's still standing!"

"Are you kidding? That kid is a great fighter. I did my best in there. It was all I could do to keep up with him."

The Punisher reacted angrily.

"If The Punisher wants things done right, The Punisher has to do them himself."

Across the gym, Gary got Johnny's attention as he made for the showers.

"Johnny, you certainly have the talent it takes to be a professional fighter."

"You liked that, huh?" Johnny replied smiling.

"We loved it. In fact, trials for the new season start in three weeks. They're going to be televised, and they're going to feature all the qualifying fighters from the try-outs."

"Do I qualify?" Johnny asked.

"Are you kidding?" Gary said, "I'd say more than most!"

"Three weeks?" Johnny questioned, considering the proposition.

"Three weeks and it promises to be brutal. Every fighter in the city wants to join the Warrior ranks. There are a lot of benefits to being a star. "

"I need time to think about it. Can I call you?"

"Take all the time you need to decide Johnny. If you want in, just show up at the first round. I'll have your name on the roster already."

"I'll give it some thought. Thanks."

Johnny headed into the locker room.

Gary turned to Sheila. She didn't seem to like Johnny's attitude about the fights.

"He'll show," Gary said confidently. "No one turns their back on a chance at fame."

Back at Huon's General Store, Johnny was working his afternoon shift alone. He was reliving the fights in his head while sweeping the floor and he didn't hear the sound of the front door opening. As he rounded the corner of the shelving a muscular thug sucker punched him and sent him reeling.

By the time Johnny got back to his feet a second figure grabbed him from behind. He pushed backward driving the guy through a rack of potato chips.

The beating continued with a third thug taking shots at Johnny. As he was on his last legs, he looked up to see The Punisher standing before him.

Looming over Johnny, The Punisher told him, "What you need to know is that The Punisher knows where you live, who you know and how to cause them a lot of pain."

Johnny coughed, and spit out the blood that was pooling up in his mouth.

"What do you want?" he asked.

The Punisher drove a big meaty fist into Johnny's stomach. Johnny doubled over in the arms of the other bad guys. They held him up so The Punisher could continue his speech.

"It seems that you might be the next big money maker for Mister Grasier. The Punisher doesn't like that idea. Warrior Fights is The Punisher's gig and one day you might have to face me in the ring! I thought you should know what kind of a beating you're in for."

The Punisher hit Johnny in the face, dropping his limp body to the floor. The bad guys put him back up on his wobbly legs.

Coughing and choking, Johnny tried to respond.

"I don't know what you're talking about. I just tried out for the TV show."

"Get this straight," the behemoth intruded again. "You will never beat me, and I will make sure you never try. Get it?"

Angry now, Johnny spit the blood from his mouth and rebelled yelling, "You know what? I'm a fighter too."

Johnny surprised them all with two shots that sent two of the thugs onto their backsides. The Punisher grabbed Johnny and threw him through a row of shelves. The other bad guys tore the place apart. Johnny didn't get up this time.

"Come on," The Punisher commanded. "Lets go!"

Shortly after they finished trashing the store and left, May Ling came in. She found the store destroyed.

"Oh no! Johnny, are you here?" she called out.

She frantically started searching around the store.

"Johnny!"

She turned to see Johnny struggling to get up from the mess. She ran to his side.

Chapter 9

Back at Grandfather's, May Ling was tending to Johnny's wounds with a warm facecloth. Grandfather was pacing the floor in front of them.

May said, "Grandfather, please sit!"

"Let me pace to find my words," he told her.

Johnny sat up on the couch and made an appeal to Grandfather.

"I know how you feel about teaching your art. I wouldn't ask again if it weren't for this. "

Grandfather stopped pacing and stood before Johnny.

"What I have learned was taught to me from the masters of the art," he explained. "They in turn learned it from their fathers and their fathers and their fathers. It is more than a way of life for the Chinese people and much more than a sport for the likes of the strong and brave. The knowledge entrusted to me is of a sacred trust. A gift, not an education. It is with trust that this art will not hurt, but help. Not to be spent in revenge and aggression, but lent in an effort to build security so that one may achieve goodness in every thing he does. I know the way of peace through defense, not through attack. It is just the opposite of what these Warrior's have shown you."

Johnny made a gesture of understanding with a nod.

"Maybe I'm not ready to learn."

"You may be ready Johnny," Grandfather said. "I see this in you. I have decided! I will teach you what it is you seek. I will show you what it is to be a true Warrior Fighter."

Through a painfully abused face, Johnny smiled. May Ling hugged him close, knowing he was truly excited.

Shortly there-after Maria came to Grandfather's house. Johnny talked with her about the events that transpired and what it was he would be doing.

"You have to be crazy Johnny!" Maria said. "What if they do this to you again? It could be worse next time."

"Mom," Johnny said, trying to calm her concerns. "The store will be closed for at least a month, and Grandfather Ling is a true master of the art. He has agreed to train me for the fights."

"You know, your father always told me that he was training you so you wouldn't have to fight. Why do you have to fight with those monsters? All they do is glorify violence!"

"Mom, I have to try," Johnny said.

Maria was flustered. She added, "I just don't understand."

Johnny did understand her worries. It was hard to explain to her that this was more than a fighting competition. This was about honor, and pride.

"I can't explain it mom, I just have to do this. I have to meet their challenge. For me, and for everything that Dad taught me to be."

There was an awkward silence between them. Maria had no say in the matter and she knew she couldn't win this battle with words. She didn't want to give up the fight, but she gave in on the conversation.

"Then go," she said. Learn what Grandfather has to teach you and come back to me, ready to be my son. When this is over, I want my son back in one piece."

"When this is over mom, I may never need to fight again."

Maria smiled and gave Johnny a hug. She said, "A mother can only dream."

Maria had brought over clothing and personal items for Johnny, as during his training, he would be living at Grandfather's house. She delivered his gear and gave him her blessings and made her way home.

Later that evening May Ling and Johnny sat on a wooden swing under one of the oak trees in Grandfather's back yard. May had her head on Johnny's shoulder.

"Grandfather tells me you fight in just over three weeks."

"Despite being sore," Johnny said, "I feel like I could take them all on this minute."

He was quite sore still.

"Being with you makes me feel strong inside May Ling."

"I feel good inside too Johnny. Since the night we met, I have felt that anything is possible."

They rocked in the swing, watching fireflies flitter in the night sky.

"May Ling," Johnny said, "I have to say something."

May sat up to look at Johnny's face.

"Tell me Johnny. Anything you want to say, I'm listening."

"May Ling, I …"

She looked deep into his eyes, right down into his heart and squeaked out, "Yes Johnny?"

In their loss for words, she leaned in to him. They shared a long kiss and an even longer hug.

May whispered, "Johnny, I am scared for you."

Johnny leaned back in the bench swing. He was scared too and wasn't afraid to admit it. This was bigger than anything he'd faced before and he wasn't completely sure he was ready.

"I'm scared too May Ling, but I feel it inside. I know I stand a chance in doing what's right."

May Ling put her head back on Johnny's shoulder. She wraps her arms around him and they simply swung in silence.

Chapter 10

At six o'clock in the morning Lap backed his station wagon up the driveway and blew his horn with a few short beeps. Grandfather came out to him from the side of the house. Johnny stepped out onto the porch in sweat pants, yawning while he pulled on a t-shirt. He'd been woken up by the sound of the car horn.

Lap greeted them and said, "Day one for Johnny, yes?"

Johnny was still in a morning haze, squinting his eyes in the rising suns light.

"I'm ready for it," he said. "What's for breakfast?"

Grandfather chuckled and said, "We will see how ready you are. Training starts now!"

Johnny raised his eyebrows and looked over to Lap and asked, "Strength training?"

Lap nodded and replied, "Yes, just like the store. You bring these bags in the house."

Doing as he was instructed, Johnny grabbed two a bags and hurried to get them indoors.

Grandfather said to Lap, "You think I have a good student in this one?"

Lap laughed, "Oh yes. Wait until you see how well he sweeps the floor."

Grandfather raised his eyebrows with interest and nodded with a 'Hmmmm'.

As with any training, the first day was tough. Grandfather was introducing Johnny to techniques he had never seen or even considered before. Grandfather brought Johnny over to a small circular pit of sand.

"This exercise is to improve speed," he explained to Johnny. "You stand in the sand."

Johnny got in the middle of the circle and asked, "Like this?"

Grandfather produced two bamboo rods. With one, he swung and hit Johnny in the shin.

"Blaaaahh! OW! That hurt!"

Johnny reached down and rubbed his shin. As he did,

Grandfather swung and hit him in the butt and knocked him out of the circle.

"You are too slow Johnny Powers!" Grandfather said laughing out loud.

"Well I didn't know you were going to hit me with sticks!"

Grandfather was still laughing as he explained, "It's just bamboo, it can't hurt you."

Johnny got back in the circle. A little perplexed, he asked, "Are you sure? It felt like it hurt to me!"

"I am quite positive," Grandfather said. "Lets do it again."

Johnny stood on guard. Grandfather poked at his leg again. Johnny stepped to avoid the bamboo. He looked down at the stick and pointed at it saying, "Ha ha!"

Grandfather tapped Johnny on the shoulder with the other stick and when he turned to see it, Grandfather swept him off his feet with the first stick.

Johnny lay on his back and look up to see the stick coming down at his head. As he raised his hands to block it, Grandfather struck him on the abdomen with the other stick.

"Ow! I just can't win!" Johnny said.

"It does not hurt," Grandfather told him.

"It still feels like it does," Johnny said with frustration.

Grandfather proposed a question.

"Why do you use two hands to stop a hollow stick?"

"Well," Johnny thought out loud, "it WAS coming straight at my head."

"But it is a hollow stick!" Grandfather said.

"I wasn't thinking about that, I guess."

Grandfather jested, "Maybe you weren't thinking at all, hmmm? This exercise is not to make your body faster, it is to make you think faster. To improve your mind."

"My mind?" Johnny questioned.

"Let me ask you this," Grandfather said. "What if those hooligans that harassed May Ling had sticks? When you stop one stick with both hands, the other hooligan can stop you with just one hand."

"Or a stick!" Johnny said, trying to be clever.

"Yes, with one stick. I will teach you to stop a hand and to be ready for a foot."

"Cool!" Johnny said with new vigor. "Lets try it again!"

"With a stick for now," Grandfather told him, "because it does not hurt."

"That's right," Johnny said. "because a stick doesn't hurt!"

"It is mind over matter young one. No pain."

Johnny perked up, ready to go. He said, "I can do this. Absolutely no pain!"

May Ling was watching from the back porch as Grandfather made his next attack on Johnny. She winced at the sound of the thin bamboo rod hitting Johnny again. She could hear him across the lawn.

"Ow! It still hurts!"

She smiled as she observed his training continue.

As the day progressed, so did Johnny's training sessions. Grandfather had brought Johnny to a group of colored circles in the grass.

"You will like this one. It is how your American game Twister got started."

"I was great at that game!" Johnny boasted with

confidence.

"You have good balance then?" Grandfather asked. "Prove this to me. I will tell you what colors to stand in, you simply do as I tell you."

"I think I can handle that," Johnny said.

"Left – Red!" Grandfather instructed. Johnny did as he was told.

"Right – Green! Left – Yellow!"

Johnny did quite well and was feeling satisfied with his balancing skills.

"So I just have to step into these circles?" he asked.

"Right," Grandfather said. "But one more thing."

Johnny was keeping his balance when he asked something he probably didn't want to know.

"What's that?" he asked.

Grandfather beaned Johnny in the forehead with a tennis ball.

Grandfather laughed and said, "Don't get hit! Red – Right!"

Johnny spun his right foot to the red circle and got hit in the back with a tennis ball. He sighed with frustration.

"This is why we practice," Grandfather told him.

Johnny offered another rebuttal stating, "There are no tennis balls in Twister!"

"Right – Yellow."

Johnny traded foot positions swiftly and ducked the ball. He smiled, beaming with pride and Grandfather hit him with yet another ball.

Johnny took the torment of not being able to out maneuver the tennis balls and he kept stepping in and out of circles for what must have been another hour.

He did start to improve.

That night, alone without Grandfather, Johnny was trying to kick down tennis balls as he threw them into the air. He did hit the occasional ball, but he was inconsistent and very frustrated. From the kitchen window May Ling and Grandfather were watching Johnny try over and over again. Grandfather kept chuckling.

"Do not laugh at his failure Grandfather, he is trying," May Ling said.

"I am not laughing at his failure May Ling. I am thrilled at his determination. I had the same troubles when I was a boy. His failure will pass quickly."

"Then you truly feel that training him is not a mistake in judgment?" she asked.

Grandfather raised his hands and stretched himself up tall, taking a deep and satisfied breath.

"A mistake? Why I haven't felt younger in years. This Johnny Powers is best thing that could have happened to an old man like me."

May Ling hugged Grandfather and said, "Thank you Grandfather."

Still acting like a grumpy old man when he received affection, he shooed May away and told her, "Okay, Okay. You go tell him it is time to sleep. Morning comes quickly."

"Okay," she said, springing out the door and into the yard. She had been instructed not to interfere in his training and she hadn't been able to be near him all day. She had been waiting patiently.

May Ling came around a row of hedges to the area where Johnny was working out on a Wooden Man. As he was striking the figure, it spun posts back at him. He blocked, struck and spun the man around and around. It was clear that his skills were improving by the hour.

"Johnny?" she called gently, not to surprise him.

He turned quickly at the sound of her voice. As he did, he spotted one of the posts spinning toward him in his peripheral vision. He stopped it his foot while facing May Ling.

"It's late, shouldn't you be asleep?" he said to her.

May was taking time off work to find a better job in a better location. She was in no hurry to get to sleep. After all, Johnny was up and she hadn't talked with him all day.

She grabbed his hand and pulled him toward the house saying, "Grandfather just said the same thing about you! Time for bed. He wants me to tell you that the morning comes quickly and you should get your rest."

"I'll be in shortly, I'd like to review a few more blocking strategies. Is that alright?"

"Okay, but I want to watch," May said.

Johnny turned back to the wooden man and began the striking and spinning over again. He was surely swift, more so now than even just a day ago.

He stopped and asked May Ling, "Has Grandfather said anything about my ability?"

"He talks about the many great things you can do," she answered.

"But has he talked at all about how 'good' I am?"

May tilted her head as if to scold Johnny. She said, "Remember? He told you that you are the best you can be if you try your hardest."

"I remember," Johnny sighed. " Try my best."

"Well, are you trying your best Johnny Powers?"

Johnny looked astonished at the question. He replied, "Of course I am!"

"Then Grandfather would only tell you that you are the best that you can be. Better comes with time."

Johnny looked up at the sky, then back down to May Ling and said with a smile, "You think just like him don't you?"

"Lucky for me I am my Grandfather's little girl, hmm?"

Johnny laughed at how she said 'Hmmm', just like Grandfather always does.

"Lucky for me too," he told her.

May jumped over the two foot space between them and put a quick 'Muah' on his face and headed back toward the house.

She called out behind herself, "Goodnight Johnny!" and she was gone in a flash.

Johnny turned back to the wooden man. He hit a few posts and tried some stuff that made him look incredibly swift. He smiled with satisfaction in his improvement.

A Story By Joe Dolan

Chapter 11

At 6:00 AM Grandfather quietly slipped into Johnny's bedroom and dropped a pair of sandals onto his stomach to wake him up. Johnny sat up rapidly and grabbed the sandals off his stomach.

"Time to wake Johnny. Long road ahead today."

Johnny rubbed his eyes and asked, "What long road is that?"

"Long road downtown! You put on these shoes and run down to the Post Office. Grandfather needs stamps."

Johnny reluctantly rolled out of bed and put on the sandals. He came downstairs wearing them with a pair of shorts and a terribly wrinkled t-shirt.

"Do I really have to wear these?" Johnny asked.

"You will hate me for them today, but next week you will thank me. Makes your legs stronger, now go get me stamps."

Grandfather handed money to Johnny.

"And I have to run?" Johnny asked.

"Oh yes," Grandfather replied. "And get two gallons of milk please. May Ling tells me we are out of milk."

Johnny stood in awe.

"I have to run with two gallons of milk?"

"And a book of stamps," Grandfather noted.

Johnny rolled his eyes and made for the door. He sighed and said, "Oh man. The Karate Kid never had it this tough."

As Johnny was making for the door, Grandfather called behind him.

"I'm not Mr. Miagi and you're not fighting the Kobra Kai!"

Johnny started to jog out the driveway. Grandfather chuckled to himself as he watched. He was quite proud of Johnny.

It was a hot and sunny day in Metropolis and the streets downtown were nearly glaring in the morning sunshine. A very sweaty Johnny came out of the post office with an envelope of stamps in his shirt pocket and a gallon of milk in each hand. He got on the sidewalk and started jogging back to the house as Grandfather came riding alongside him on a beach-cruiser bicycle with a big wicker basket on the handlebars.

Johnny kept jogging and turned his head to face Grandfather. He didn't break his stride.

"Johnny," Grandfather said, "I felt bad for making you run with so many things. I came to offer some assistance."

Johnny stopped with a grateful smile.

"Really?" he asked.

Grandfather nodded with an understanding look on his face. After a moment he pointed into the basket on the front of the bike.

"You may put the stamps in the basket," he said.

Johnny looked down at the basket, up at Grandfather and down at the two gallons of milk he was holding. He bent at the waist and put the milk on the ground. He stood back up and took the stamps in the little white envelope from his pocket.

"Go ahead," Grandfather said.

Johnny put the envelope into the basket.

"See you at the house," Grandfather said as he casually pedaled away. Johnny watched Grandfather for a moment as he left and Grandfather raised his hand and waved for Johnny to follow, never turning around to see if he was coming.

Laughing to himself and shaking his head in disbelief, Johnny picked up the milk and followed. He had now learned to expect the unexpected in everything Grandfather does.

After lunch and a rest, Johnny and Grandfather spent the day working on striking and blocking maneuvers in the yard. Occasionally they would break for May Ling's freshly squeezed lemonade.

Chapter 12

Behind Grandfather's house he had built a very nice dojo. Red mats on the floor, dark wood lining the walls and a great stereo system for enjoying music while he exercised. Grandfather invited Johnny into the dojo for the first time since his arrival and Johnny was quite beside himself for the opportunity to be invited in.

When they got inside, Grandfather walked to a table on the far side of the room and he lit two candles. Johnny's interest was peaked.

"You have come a long way through these weeks of lessons Johnny. Now it is time for a lesson in effort."

Grandfather pointed to the candles.

"Once, when I was your age, my teacher lit two candles and showed me this."

Grandfather pulled up his sleeve and concentrated for a second, then with a quick whip of his hand, he pushed his palm toward the candle and the flame 'popped' and went out without a flicker. Johnny was impressed with the accuracy.

Grandfather shook his head and said, "This is what I show to him."

Grandfather leaned over and blew the other candle out with a minimal breath. Johnny was astounded.

"What did he do after you blew out the candle?" Johnny asked.

"He presented me with my next belt," Grandfather told him.

Johnny smiled wide in hopes that this was his belt test. Grandfather stood out in the middle of the dojo floor and gestured for Johnny to come closer.

"Now you show me something."

Johnny stepped onto the mat with Grandfather.

Grandfather pointed at the mat and said, "Lap tells me you know a lot about sweeping the floor. This floor needs some attention."

Johnny's jaw dropped because he was expected a lesson in fighting. Grandfather made no movement to signal that this was a joke so Johnny went over to the closet door where a broom was leaning against the wall. He picked up the broom, then opened the closet door and put the broom inside. He pulled out a vacuum cleaner instead.

Grandfather put a wide smile on his face. He approached Johnny while he plugged the vacuum's cord into the wall. Reaching into the closet, Grandfather pulled down a shoebox sized package.

"You have earned this Johnny Powers," he told him.

Opening the box, he presented Johnny with the Black Belt that was folded inside. Johnny was wide eyed and happy.

"Is this the belt your teacher gave you?" he asked Grandfather excitedly.

"My goodness no!" Grandfather barked. He pointed to a display on the far wall with a sword and a belt encased in a shadowbox.

"That is the belt my teacher gave me! This is the belt your teacher is giving you. I bought it yesterday when I rode the bike downtown."

Grandfather threw his hands dramatically in the air and shook his head and he said, "You watch too many karate movies on TV."

Grandfather opened the door and stepped outside, leaving Johnny in the dojo with the vacuum. Johnny called behind him.

"Thank you Grandfather."

Johnny could hear Grandfather reply from out in the yard.

"Thank me by vacuuming the floor. Then you come in for dinner, hmmmm?"

Johnny did just that.

May Ling, Johnny and Grandfather sat and talked over dinner.

"Tomorrow is the first match May Ling. Will you be watching?"

"We will both be watching, right Grandfather?" May said.

Grandfather nodded in agreement while he ate.

"It's just against the other competitors trying to make it up the ranks," Johnny said. "It still promises to have a lot of action though!"

Between bites Grandfather spoke.

"Relax yourself. You don't want to spill out everything you have on your first match."

"I just plan to win Grandfather, that's all," Johnny said confidently.

"Against amateurs? I know you will, but you must be calm and collected. Keep focus on good defense and quick attack."

"I'll do that for sure," Johnny assured him.

Grandfather finished another bite of his noodle dish.

"Then you will do just fine."

Chapter 13

At the Warrior Fights Arena cameras were set up all over the gym. The seats were fairly well filled, but not like the fights when the Warriors were in the ring.

Johnny came into the gym with his fighting outfit already on. He looked more aware of his surroundings than the last time he was there.

Sheila saw him enter and grabbed Gary's shoulder, directing his attention to Johnny.

"Whaddya know? The Golden Boy showed up after all."

Gary's head spun to see Johnny.

"Well, well, well," he said. "Dressed up and ready to kill. I'll go have a word with him."

Gary got up from the table they sat at and approached Johnny.

"Johnny Powers! Come to join us in the fun and games?"

Johnny wasn't so green this time. He was sure and confident and Gary could see this.

"I came to throw my hat in the ring," Johnny said. "Sure."

"I was hoping that you would have called us about showing up. You know, the press is going to love that you're here."

"I'm not looking for any special treatment, I just want to fight," Johnny said.

"You'll get that chance," Gary told him, "but I must say, there are going to be a lot of disappointed fighters here today."

Johnny raised his eyebrows and asked, "Why is that?"

"Johnny, I've seen you fight. Some of these unknowns thought they had a chance today, but with you here…"

Gary shrugged his shoulders.

"You've got some faith in me Mr. Graiser."

Gary winked and pointed 'gun-fingers' at Johnny.

"Knock 'em dead kid. Literally."

He returned to the table as Johnny headed for the locker room. He grabbed Sheila's attention.

"Get every paper and TV reporter we know on the line and tell them that we have Johnny Powers down here right now. Headline, Johnny Powers wants to go for the Championship Belt!"

"Miles ahead of you," she said. "I have the office on it already."

Gary leaned over and kissed Sheila on the cheek.

"I can see the press already. Golden Boy Johnny Powers takes on the Warrior Fighters. Every station is going to carry this one."

"But what if he loses? We didn't set anything up," Sheila asked.

Gary laughed. "Ha, against the unknowns? Never going to happen. But don't worry. We'll make sure he stays in this when he goes up to the big leagues, don't you worry. For now, let's just enjoy the show."

When show time came around Johnny found himself sitting along a short set of bleachers with all of the other contenders. The Punisher walked by and spotted Johnny. He offered Johnny a cold stare and a grunt as he passed.

"Didn't have enough last time punk? Try and make it to the big ring! I'll be waiting!" The Punisher said to him.

Johnny was calm and completely unfazed by the verbal attack. He just looked past The Punisher and at the ring. Without an immediate response, The Punisher got frustrated and stormed off.

All of the other fighters within an earshot looked at Johnny with surprise and suspicion. A Metropolis gang member named Peace sat next to Johnny.

"I take it that you two know each other on a personal level?" Peace asked.

"Fortunately not!" Johnny said.

"Well, even though I now know who your enemies are, I'm still willing to introduce myself. I'm Nick Thompson. They call me Peace."

Johnny asked, "Do you belong to a gang?

"Yeah, the Saviors. We're not a gang, like a bad gang, we try to keep an eye on the streets at night."

"Does it work?" Johnny asked.

"We can only do so much," Peace said with a chuckle. He took a closer look at Johnny.

"Hey, you're the Power!"

Johnny was starting to regret having a name that was so easy to abuse. He replied, "I'm Johnny Powers, yeah."

"Yeah, Johnny Powers. No offense meant with the nickname, that's what they call you at the clubhouse. We've got a picture of you up for inspiration. You know, lone civilian does good for the community!"

"Thanks, I think. I didn't know I had that affect on people."

"Yeah, you're like our hero. We feel that if more citizens did what you did, we could relax a little more at night."

Johnny huffed and replied, "I think if more people tried to do that, we'd have more casualties to deal with, don't you?"

"I guess so." Peace Shrugged. "So do you know when you're fighting?"

A Bell rang and all heads turned to an electronic board that illuminated with two names.

The board read: SPIKE vs. POWERS.

Johnny stood up.

"I guess I'm first. Wish me luck."

Peace knocked knuckles with him and said, "Show 'em what you've got!"

Johnny got in the ring and his opponent Spike was jumping around like a deranged monkey.

"Kill you man! Kill you!" Spike taunted.

Johnny looked out of the ring at Peace who just shrugged his shoulders at the ordeal. Johnny shook his head and chuckled.

The ring announcer came on the microphone and the cameras lit up with red dome lights to signify the feed was live.

"Ladies and gentlemen in the arena and viewers at home. Welcome to the Warrior Fights arena. Today begins the first of two days of non-stop action on our very own Channel 5. Over one hundred fighters from across the Country have gathered here to try their skills in the ring and to earn their chance to compete on Warrior Fights."

The crowd lit up with hoots and hollers.

"For our first fight tonight, squaring off we have in the left corner – contender Spike!"

Spike jumped around and yelled while pointing into the live cameras.

"In the right corner we have the Golden Boy, as seen on Channel Five News. The Savior, The Hero, The Power – Mister Johnny Powers!"

The audience was just now hearing the name and they were brought to their feet when they heard it. Johnny looked out and saw the fans standing and cheering. For the first time realized that this was really going to be a big event. He knew he had to give his all.

"As each fighter scores a win, he will be moved up the ranks in his group. The top of each group will fight each other until two fighters remain. They will each have a chance to fight in the Warriors ring just one week from tonight! Fighters know the rules as far as their opponent goes, it is bare hand fighting until your opponent quits, or is stopped by forcible measure. Now, without further hesitation, let the games begin!"

The lights in the seating areas dimmed and the crowd went wild. Spotlights focused on the ring and the action was about to start.

At home, May Ling and Grandfather were tuned in to the television.

"He looks ready Grandfather," May said eagerly.

"For amateurs, he is ready," Grandfather stated. "He still has some lessons to learn, but today, he will be fine."

The Referee signaled for the fighters to stand on their marks.

Johnny showed no emotion as he stared into the face of Spike. Spike was already sweaty and tense. Johnny, however, was cool and collected.

"Bring on the action!" the Ref yelled as he stepped out from between the fighters.

Spike came at Johnny with a swing from the left and Johnny just moved aside and let it go by. Then came a swing from the right. Again, Johnny stepped aside. Perturbed, Spike ran forward and leapt in the air with a high sprung kick. Johnny ducked and Spike sailed right over him.

"You're the big bad hero they talk about on the news?" Spike yelled.

He taunted Johnny by sticking his chin out. He pointed to it and said, "Just hit me hero."

Like an electric switch turned on, Johnny drove an uppercut into Spikes chin and it lifted his body two feet off the mat. Spike was unconscious before he dropped into a heap on the ring mat.

The audience was silent with awe and the ref stood and stared down at Spike for a second. He blew his whistle and hoisted Johnny's hand in the air.

"Winner of the match by a clear cut knockout – Johnny Powers!"

The room was still silent and in awe.

Peace yelled, "Powers!"

Johnny turned toward Peace and the silent crowd. Then the room erupted in cheer.

At Grandfather's house May was bouncing up and down on the couch and clapping. Grandfather smiled and nodded with pride.

Johnny climbed under the ropes and sat back down next to Peace without a word.

Peace turned to him and said, "Well, that was different."

Johnny smiled and nodded and leaned his head back against the wall. The big board flashed again.

PEACE VS. The Big K.O.

"The Big K.O. huh?" Johnny remarked.

Peace said, looking up at the board, "This should be interesting."

"Give 'em hell," Johnny said.

Peace climbed into the ring like a veteran fighter. It was clear by his posture and confidence that he'd been in a number of scuffs before and this didn't worry him one bit.

The Big K.O. climbed in behind him and he watched as he strutted by. The fighters stood in their respective corners and the Ref centered himself in the ring.

After the announcement, the Ref met the boys in the middle of the ring. He asked, "Are you ready?"

Neither responded. They just held their stare-down.

The Ref shouted out, "Bring on the action!"

A number of throws were given and strikes traded between the two for just about a minutes time. At the 55 second mark Peace showed he had the upper hand and in a series of straight to the head punches, The Big K.O. was exactly what he claimed to be. A Big Knock Out.

The Ref held Peace by the wrist and lifted his hand in victory.

Peace climbed out of the ring and sat next to Johnny. Johnny has his head against the wall, eyes closed.

"Round one," Peace said.

Johnny smiled, still with his eyes closed. He repeated it back to peace, "Round One."

Peace also leaned back against the wall with his eyes closed and the two sat for a few seconds without words. Then Johnny piped up with a laugh.

"Bad-ass!"

They laughed and laughed and laughed as the next two fighters were called to the ring.

Gary was upstairs in the office with a telephone in each hand.

"Yes, one hit." He shouted. "Weren't you watching? This kid is going to wow them at the finals. How much do you want to wager?"

Sheila came into the room and watched Gary work the two phones.

"I say we keep it small until he gets in the ring with The Punisher. No, nobody will know. For a small piece of the action, any one of our boys will take a fall. I guarantee it!"

Gary held the phones out in front of his mouth.

"Sure, I guarantee it. Two Million? I think we can count on it Mister Lee. Okay. "

Gary hung up one of the phones. Into the other phone he yelled, "Did you get all that? Good!"

He proceeded to hang up the other phone and turned to Sheila.

"Did you say two million?" she asked with a grin.

"With a twenty percent cut, that makes us a cool four hundred thousand dollars, tax free and clear."

"Baby, you just melt me with that kind of talk," she said.

Gary jumped up from behind his desk and looked out the bay window down onto the arena.

"Call Blade up here will you? We have to set up some matches for our Golden Boy."

As the fights continued Johnny watched with little interest. Through the series of matches Johnny's name was posted quite often on the board. His speed and agility won every time.

At the end of program's trials, Johnny was in the ring for his final match with a fighter named Claw.

The ref got on the microphone to announce the match.

"This match will decide the last of our finalists for the day. Fighters on their mark."

He signaled the fighters to begin.

Claw caught Johnny with a blow to the chest right off. Johnny wasn't caught off guard however, he took the hit and he hit back, hard!

A wild series of kicks and punches flew back and forth but none really connected. It looked like it was going to go the full five minutes.

Apart for a moment, the two fighters regained composure. Johnny looked at the fighter before him and kicked at his shoulder. As the fighter grabbed the kick, Johnny drove his left fist into his opponent's groin. Claw dropped like a brick.

The Ref ran in with his hands raised. The fight was over and Johnny was announced on live television that he would be a competitor in the finals round."

May Ling couldn't have been more excited, and

Grandfather was digging into the last of a big bowl of popcorn on his corner of the couch.

"He won Grandfather, Johnny won!" May shouted out loud.

With a smug pride, grandfather responded.

"I taught him that defense the first night I met him. Is there any more popcorn?

May Ling jumped off the couch and yelled to the TV screen.

"Whoo-hoo Johnny. I love you, I loooove you."

Grandfather stopped digging into the bowl and looked up at her with a blank stare.

Now having professed her love out loud in front of Grandfather, she expected a negative response from him. She turned and looked at him staring up from the couch at her.

He questioned May Ling with an odd look, then he asked, "I'll make more popcorn, is that okay?"

She turned back to the screen and continued jumping up and down and cheering.

It was late when Johnny came into the house. He looked tired. May Ling ran to him and hugged him tightly.

"I spoke to your mother on the telephone. She is very proud of you Johnny."

"Thank you. I'm really wiped out, I'll call her tomorrow."

Grandfather came into the room.

"I told you it would be a piece of cake. Nothing but amateurs."

Johnny dropped his bag to the floor and voiced a weary opinion.

"Tough amateurs though."

"Next time you will finish quicker and stronger," Grandfather told him.

"You Promise?" Johnny asked.

"Yes I do. Now, as a reward for your achievements, you get to sleep late tomorrow."

Johnny smiled with thanks.

"Instead of six o'clock," Grandfather let him know, "I will wake you at six-fifteen. Goodnight."

Grandfather turned and marched off to bed.

May stood as close to Johnny as she could. She expressed, "You looked great on TV today. I recorded it for you."

"Thank you," Johnny said, kissing her once and growing weaker by the minute. "I'm off to sleep."

May turned off the lights and went off to her own room for the night too.

Chapter 12

Johnny started the day in the set of colored rings with Grandfather throwing tennis balls at him.

"Step outside of the circles and stand prepared to fight," Grandfather instructed. Johnny did as he was told.

"Show me blocking patterns"

As Johnny started his blocks, Grandfather threw tennis balls in his way. Johnny swatted them aside like they are mere leaves falling from the sky. His accuracy was fine.

"You do well when they come slowly. Lets try them faster."

Grandfather threw them much more aggressively and he got several of them, though some sailed by.

"It comes with time Johnny, and today we will take the time."

Johnny agrees with a nod.

Grandfather stood before Johnny and they connected with a two man form, practicing both blocks and strikes. The moved with a precise fluidity, training Johnny's muscles to react in a specific manner. He was closer than ever to the perfection that Grandfather hoped for him to achieve. As this carried on Johnny continued to improve.

At the W.F.C. Office Gary was working the numbers at his desk when Sheila came in with some paperwork. She was pretty worked up about it.

"Ratings were even higher than expected," she pointed out. "They climbed as the day went on and the network thinks it's because of Johnny Powers."

Gary leaned back in his chair and put his hands over his head.

"That's our boy," he beamed. "We have the ratings now and were going to make a killing on commercial time. "

"How are plans for making our Golden Boy look real good?" Sheila asked.

"I've considered the fighters that we have for the next bout and I think there is only one fighter who has a chance against Johnny."

Sheila chimed in agreeing. She asked, "You mean Peace?"

"That's the one! He's not a bad fighter at all."

"How does he feel about money?"

"I'll have to pay him a visit and see. Can we get fifty thousand cash before noontime today?"

"I'll see to it," Sheila said.

"We're going to buy us a loser today," Gary stated confidently.

Grandfather had run out of tennis balls in his bucket and they were all over the yard waiting to be raked up. He decided it was as good a time as any for a rest.

"Time to take a drink and breathe. Taking time to rest the body and mind are important. We breathe to achieve balance between them. Do this now and I will get some cool water."

Johnny sat and meditated. While he did, May Ling crept up behind him. She threw her arms around him and he flipped her over his shoulder harmlessly onto the grass in front of him.

"You shouldn't be interrupting lessons," Johnny said laughing. " Grandfather might get upset."

"It's okay," she said. "I have to tell you something."

His laughing became serious.

"What is it May Ling?"

She moved closer and laid across Johnny's lap. She looked up at a boy who was just out to grab a pizza when he came into the life of a girl who just wanted to meet him, even though she had no idea that he existed. She smiled and ran her hand over his head.

"I love you Johnny Powers."

Johnny was silent.

"I hope I did not say something wrong," she said.

Johnny broke out of his stare and said, "No no. Not at all."

"The other day, when I kissed you, I thought that you were going to tell me you have fallen in love with me. I hope I wasn't wrong."

"May Ling," Johnny said with a warm smile. "I am in love with you. I fell in love with you the first time I saw your face. It's just that this is the first time I have ever heard these words from a girl who wasn't my mother and well, …"

"Well?" May asked.

"Wow!" Johnny said. Then he said it louder. "WOW!"

May pulled him closer for a kiss when Grandfather came around the edge of the house with a garden hose and doused them completely.

They yelled with laughter and surprise. As they tried to get to their feet Grandfather chased them and squirted them some more.

"Grandfather!" May shouted while she laughed and ran in circles.

"Pitching woo with my Granddaughter? Here is your cold drink Mister Powers," Grandfather said laughing out loud.

Johnny scooped his hands together and threw some of the water back at Grandfather.

"You think I am afraid to get wet do you?" Grandfather asked. He turned the hose on himself.

"Now you!" he shouted at Johnny.

This carried on for a while as Johnny settled into the acceptance that they would be, from this moment on, more than just friends. He would one day marry this girl and Grandfather would become his own family.

He thought at that moment that everything in the universe was right as it should be.

Across town, however, Gary Grasier walked up the steps of the home that Peace lived in. Blade stood beside him as he knocked on the door.

Peace answered the door.

"Mister Grasier? Blade?" he said with surprise.

"Hi Peace," Gary said. "Can we talk?"

A little unsure as to what they wanted, Peace let them into the house.

At Grandfathers, things were dried off and lessons were back on. Johnny was filled with a new vigor and it showed in everything he did. He was almost at the completion of his training for this fight. Grandfather stood before him with some instructions.

"Now is the time to channel all your energy into defense. Follow Grandfather."

Johnny was curious and followed Grandfather into a clay tennis court off to the back of the property. In the fenced in court he spotted a tennis ball launcher.

"You are kidding me!" he said.

"No," Grandfather assured him. "Not at all. This is the best workout I have."

Johnny was leery, but he followed Grandfather into the caged in court.

"You turn it on," Grandfather told him.

Grandfather made his way to the far side of the court in direct line of the machine.

"I'm ready," Johnny shouted.

Grandfather raised a waving hand and called back, "Give it to me!"

Johnny turned on the machine. It wasn't at full speed, but it was churning out the balls one after another.

Grandfather effortlessly swatted them down with his hands and his feet. A youthful stride in every move he made, it was a rare glimpse for Johnny, or anyone, to see a true master of the art in full speed practice.

After a minute or so Grandfather stepped out of the line of fire and Johnny shut the machine off.

"Now you."

Johnny got in front of the machine. As he was walking to the distant side of he court Grandfather turned it on and launched a tennis ball toward Johnny's back. Johnny twisted away. The ball missed.

"Hey!"

Grandfather hid his chuckle.

"Oops. Sorry."

Johnny shook off his doubt and prepared himself, though with a small amount of trepidation. He stood ready for the onslaught.

"Go ahead," Johnny said, like Grandfather did. "Give it to me."

Grandfather turned the machine on. Johnny started to deflect the balls as fast as they came. There had to be thousands of them ready to fire from the machine across from Johnny. This wasn't going to be over in the next few minutes.

Grandfather kicked the machine up a notch and made his way out of the court. The machine churned out ball after ball.

"Think of me as the Terminator while I'm gone," he yelled

to Johnny.

"I don't get it. How is that?"

Grandfather yelled to him once more.

"Ill be back."

As this made Johnny laugh he lost his focus and got pinged with a couple of balls.

He yelled back, "That's not funny!"

When father came back to the house he found Peace standing on the porch. He introduced himself and asked if Grandfather could offer him a few minutes to talk without Johnny around.

Grandfather invited him inside for tea.

Sitting at the table, Peace explained the situation.

"I don't mean to bother you at home sir, but I have to tell you what is going on. If I hadn't met Johnny, I suppose I might have taken the money, but Johnny stands for things I believe in. He stands up for the rights of people who can't stand up for themselves. I respect that."

"What did they tell you," Grandfather asked.

"They have this thing with viewer ratings where they boost a character's popularity and then set them up to lose. They take bets and everybody makes money on it, and they said if Johnny stays in the show they're sure to make even more. Gary Grasier says he will set up a two million dollar bet against me for my match with Johnny. They want me to throw the match. I mean, they want it to look good, but they want Johnny to win."

"And he will," Grandfather said confidently.

"I've watched him fight, I know that. Still, I can't just throw it away. I know it's most likely I'll lose to Johnny, but I may never get a chance to fight someone that great in a televised competition ever again. I have to give my all."

"It is with deepest respect that I thank you for this information Mister Thompson. Please, give Johnny the best workout you can, but do not speak of this to him, or to anybody else on this matter until the fight has ended."

"You have my word Mister Ling. I will keep this a secret at all cost."

Peace said all he had to and knew he was taking time from Johnny's training. He readily dismissed himself.

As he thanked Grandfather, Johnny was visible from the porch, working out with the tennis ball machine. Peace looked in awe.

"Wow!", he said with his jaw open.

"Are you impressed?" Grandfather asked.

"Actually sir, I'm a little frightened."

Grandfather patted Peace on the shoulder as he turned to leave and get some practice in for himself.

A Story By Joe Dolan

Chapter 13

The W.F.C. Arena was lit up with bright lights and excitement. This time there were less fighters and more spectator seats. The results from today's events would decide the fate of one fighter.

Johnny didn't look nervous at all as he stretched along a wall away from cameras. Peace came across the arena and joined him.

"How's it going buddy?" Peace asked.

Johnny looked up from his stretching.

"Hey Peace. Ready to fight today?"

He was really tense with all that was going on but he didn't let on at all to Johnny.

"Ready as I'll ever be. Mind if I stretch over here? There seems to be a little more privacy."

Johnny sprang to his feet.

"You're my brother Nick. You're always welcome."

They high fived and shared a bro-hug. Johnny and Peace used team techniques to stretch and ready themselves for the action.

On the other side of the gym Gary, Sheila and Blade looked over the layout and took account of the fighters in attendance. Gary spoke with a very serious intent to Blade.

"This promises to be a hit with the viewers. If Johnny looks good in this win, we are guaranteed the top slot next week. Commercial time is proposed at three hundred thousand dollars a minute."

"So make this look good!" Sheila demanded.

Blade nodded in agreement and headed off to the Warriors locker area. Gary looked as if he couldn't be happier.

"I just love that Johnny Powers," he said.

The arena quickly packed to capacity. The fighters were spread out on either side of the ring. The cameras sprang to life and the lights dimmed in the arena seating sections. They were live!

A microphone snapped to life with the announcer's voice.

"Ladies and gentlemen may I have your attention please. Grasier Productions and Channel Five are proud to present tonight, to a sold out capacity crowd and to millions of viewers worldwide, what has been called the most anticipated fight to happen in the history of the Warrior Fights program."

As the Announcer gave his spiel the fighters warmed up individually.

"The Inner City Showdown Spectacular!"

Many looks were passed from one face to the next as some fighters tried to inspire fear and intimidation, while others simply hoped to get their chance to shine without to rough of a beating.

The bell rang and contender board flashed:

PEACE vs. CRUSH

Without words, Peace stood from stretching with Johnny and made his way into the ring. Cameras followed his every step. Crush entered the ring from the other side. They both looked to be more serious and dedicated fighters than the previous televised batch.

The fight began. A terrific opening match for the

program, both Peace and Crush seemed equally capable of handling their own in the martial arts world. Blow by blow, kick and strike met with little debilitating effect on either of the fighters. At the four minute mark though, Peace kicked it up a notch. It was almost as if he'd been waiting for his prey to weaken and was playing a weaker fighter than he truly was.

Crush came across the ring and swung full force at Peace. Peace took the punch to the upper chest and stood like Superman, completely unfazed. Then the tables turned against Crush.

Peace walked toward Crush. Crush took an intimidated step back as he looked in horror. Peace was like a robot. He pushed the space between them back until Crush met the turnbuckle. Then all hell broke loose.

A left upper-cut. A right hook. A series of nearly 15 straight jabs over and over and over until Crush was pulverized by the pummeling. His feet slid out from under him and he dropped to the floor by the ring post.

The match was over. Peace stood victorious.

The audience went wild. As Peace stepped out of the ring the media gathered in front of him.

"Tell us Peace," a reporter asked, "do you fear that you might get pitted against Johnny Powers?"

"Are you kidding? I look forward to it. He's a real competitor."

He turned and walked away. As he did the camera crew backed off.

Peace took a seat next to Johnny in the competitor stands. There was a moment's silence and Peace spoke up.

"I meant that in a good way." he said.

Johnny smiled and put his hand out to Peace. Peace gave him a quick low five.

Gary sat pleased, watching with anticipation.

The bell rang and the sign lit up: POWER vs. ANGEL.

Johnny climbed into the ring. He looked up at the sign, then down at Gary. He mouthed the words,

"It's Powers … with an S."

Gary just gave a shoulder shrug as if he didn't have anything to do with it and gave a thumbs up. Johnny dismissed it and focused on the match.

Angel looked like a tough competitor. Johnny was

smooth and he performed with a consistent attack and defense. That fluidity he gained from working with the tennis ball machine proved positive as he swatted away strike after strike being delivered by Angel.

At one moment, during his flurry of attacks, Angel reeled back to get a breath in and Johnny took advantage of the moment. He led in left handed and drove a jab, another jab and a backhand to Angels face. As it knocked him back Johnny jumped up in the air and came straight down with a driving right handed blow to Angel's forehead and ended the match in a minute.

Not waiting for applause or an announcement, Johnny made for the ropes and stepped out of the ring. He ignored the cameras and walked back to where he was sitting before the match, plopping down and leaning against the wall.

"I guess it's you and me buddy," he said to Peace.

Peace smiled. He replied, "Off the record, I'm eager to get in there and give you a workout."

Johnny nodded. He looked over at Peace and asked, "And on the record?"

Peace put his mouth guard in and grunted.

"Grrrrr!"

The two laughed and stood up to answer the barrage of press affiliates that were approaching with cameras and microphones. Some exhibition fighting was going to take place for the next hour of the ring time.

In the Warrior Team's locker room The Punisher was pacing the floor while Blade pulled on his leather television outfit. Some other Bad Guy Warriors were there too.

"That punk thinks he's going all the way, but The Punisher has some news for him."

Blade piped up.

"Come on man. The crowd has never been this big before. This kid is hot."

"Shut it!" the Punisher yelled. "This weasel has to drop, and if he gets in the big ring, The Punisher has some news for him. I'll make sure he never gets up on his own two legs again."

"Give it a rest man, this is TV.," Blade told him. "The sky is big enough for a few more stars."

The Punisher grabbed Blade by the outfit and pushed him into the row of lockers.

"I'm the star! Get it? There are no other stars in the God damned sky!"

Blade kept his composure and said, "There's something you need to remember. One of these days you might face me in the ring again."

The Punisher stood tall in an attempt to loom over blade.

"Yeah," he said. "What then?"

Blade casually ripped the door of his locker with one hand and dropped it at The Punisher's feet.

"Let's just say I don't need the money now, so I won't lose quite as easily as our last match."

Blade put one hand on The Punisher's chest and pushed his body backwards. Losing balance and stumbling back into the opposing row of lockers, the Punisher was speechless. So where his cohorts.

Blade walked toward the exit door of the locker room and he turned back.

"One more thing. Your name is Larry. Would you please stop referring to yourself in first person narrative. It makes The Punisher sound like an idiot."

Blade disappeared back out into the arena.

The Punisher was mad. Really mad.

"I'll fix that runt Johnny Powers so the last thing he'll be thinking about is what The Punisher … The Larry … I'm just going to kick his lily white ass from here to the moon!"

Johnny was completely unaware of what was going on in the locker room. He was standing in the ring across from the only person in the room he felt he could trust … and he had to kick the crap out of him.

Blade was outside the ring, shaking hands with some fans and getting a little camera time. The lights flickered to signal the start of the match and people rushed to their seats. Cameras turned to the ring and the microphone crackled to life with the voice of the announcer.

"Ladies and gentlemen. This match will decide who faces off in the big ring with the Warriors for Rumble Royale!"

The crowd applauded wildly.

"In this corner, climbing his way up through the fighting ranks, a repeat contender from the unknowns, Peace!"

In response to the applause, Peace made little action to glorify himself. He didn't showboat, but this WAS his one shot in life to be on TV and he wanted to be able to relive the glory every time he saw the broadcast recording.

"And in this corner. You've seen him on Channel Five News and he's ready to fight tonight, it's Johnny Powers."

Camera bulbs flashed and screams were loud in the air. People cheered his name through the whistles and claps.

The fighters came to the middle of the ring.

"You two ready to get it on?" the Ref asked.

The boys nodded in agreement.

"This is national boys, so make it a good one," the Ref told them.

As they 'touched gloves', Peace asked Johnny, "Give me your best, alright?"

"You too," Johnny said.

They 'touched gloves', so to say, and went to their corners. With the clang of a bell fate would be decided.

Peace resembled his nickname more than anyone you would ever meet. His life, since he was a kid, was spent righting wrongs. He was raised in an orphanage on the dirty downtown Metropolis streets, scrapping for food and begging for change. As he got older, he became the

146

protective big brother to the kids who were funneled into the orphanage behind him. He'd spent the best of his years to date going without for the benefit of others and in his heart of hearts he knew this was how he wanted to exist. It was his purpose for living, to take opportunity and give it to those who deserve it. Still, the thrill of televised fame is enough to bring out the best in anyone and he felt this was a chance for him to leave a legacy that might last and inspire people after he was gone.

The match was intended to follow the typical rules of the previous matches. Within five minutes, one man would be standing and one man would be lying on the mat, knocked out or having submitted to the other fighter. Johnny didn't see how this match could be like that. How could he do that to someone he trusted?

He shut off conscience and turned on the machine he built inside. No faces and no names. There was one option, he was either to be the best or nothing at all. That was all that mattered.

For nearly four minutes, the boys battled back and forth. Pulling no punches and no cheap shots. They displayed to the world what professionalism was and what the Warriors lacked.

Nearing the match's end, Johnny put Peace on the mat. He backed away and gave Peace a moment to recover. The crowd screamed for a dirty and violent act to end the fight, but that wasn't how Johnny played the game. He waited.

Once Peace was on his feet, Johnny got the best of him again. Peace had given his all, but even at that he fell just short of what Johnny could offer. Peace went down again.

One final blow from Johnny standing over Peace would have put his lights out. The cameras turned to Johnny and the Ref got alongside him waiting to call the match, but Johnny just stood with his arm cocked waiting for Peace to stand up and reset. The audience turned rowdy and yelled for the victory but Johnny waited.

Peace was truly beaten. He got up on one knee and reached down to tap out on the mat. He gave in for the match. The Ref signaled that Johnny was the winner, and Johnny stepped over to Peace to see that he was okay. He grabbed his arm and pulled him to his feet, raising his hand to commemorate his efforts and give him the notoriety he deserved. This was true sportsmanship.

Grandfather and May Ling watched the match on television. Grandfather nodded in favor of Johnny's actions.

"You have brought your Grandfather a true champion."

At Johnny's house, breaking glass shattered on the floor

as a big fist came through the window and reached in to unlock the door. As the door opened, in came The Punisher and his cohorts.

He commended to the Band of Nasties, "Wreck this place!"

They did as they were told.

As the guys overturned furniture and destroyed heirlooms, The Punisher looked over at the mantle.

He muttered under his breath, "What do we have here?"

He stepped up to the picture of Johnny's father and saw the Medal. With a smash from his fist, he destroyed the glass case and took the Medal of Honor.

Chapter 14

In the locker room Johnny and Peace were in the corner talking in hushed tones.

"They offered you how much?" Johnny asked.

"Fifty-thousand dollars to take a fall and guarantee you would win."

Johnny mulled it over for a moment.

"To throw the match to me?"

"Yeah."

"Did you?" Johnny asked angrily.

Peace leaned back in surprise that Johnny even asked him that.

"Yeah, if only. Buddy, you kicked my butt fair and square."

Johnny had to agree. He knew Peace wasn't holding back either. He still had to wonder what was going on.

"Why are they trying to set me up? "

Peace explained.

"They bet on the fighters. Not just small stuff you know, I mean tons of cash. They figure that if they can get you into the ring with The Punisher, you're sure to lose. They'll bet on it big time too."

"I've seen him fight," Johnny said. "I've FELT what he has to offer."

Peace reassured him and said, "And man, I've seen you fight, and I think you have a good chance at winning. I'd even bet on that."

"I would too, now." Johnny said. "You know, that kind of money could help Mr. Huon after what The Punisher did."

"So what are we going to do?" Peace asked. "I turned Gary down."

Johnny thought for a minute. Had it really all been a set-up to play on his good deeds for profit? Did he really stand a chance against The Punisher? He knew in his heart of hearts that he was at his peak physical and mental strength and for what it was worth to him, backing down was NOT an answer.

"At the very least, I'm going to win," he said confidently.

Peace grabbed his hand and pulled him over and gave him a big hug.

"You've got this one brother and I've got your back. No holds barred!" Peace told Johnny. "No holds barred!"

Gary was coming down the stairs with a briefcase. He passed some of the camera people with his fake smile on and he crossed the arena to the locker room. As he got to the doors, Johnny was coming out. He took Gary by surprise.

"Johnny! Hey, I thought you had gone already."

"I'm just leaving now," Johnny said.

"Listen," Gary babbled and fumbled his scheming words with his shyster personality. "You did it Johnny. You have proven to be the best fighter from the streets of Metropolis. I want you to know that the big fight is going to be the biggest event we've ever done on TV."

"Sounds terrific.," Johnny replied, rolling his eyes.

"C'mon buddy. You are the Golden Boy. You're making this sport the most popular thing on television."

"Look," Johnny said, stopping Gary in his tracks. "I just wanted to know what the schedule for the big match is. Do I really get to go up against The Punisher, or what?."

Gary sighed, happy that he asked. He replied, "That's what this is all about Johnny. You get a shot at what every fighter in the city wants. You get to go for the title."

Johnny still hadn't made eye contact with Gary. He was hearing everything Gary had to say but he had kept his stare at the floor and on the far wall. Gary enjoyed this as it made him feel superior.

Johnny inhaled and pulled his bag onto his shoulder and stepped up close to Gary, staring straight into his eyes.

"I can't wait!" he said.

Gary stepped back a bit in surprise. He thought for sure Johnny was under control, but for the first time he could see that Johnny wasn't a push-over.

"So you won't back out of fighting The Punisher?"

"Not a chance."

"Well alright then," Gary said with a smile. "You will have your big chance, and I'm willing to bet that the Punisher would like a chance in the ring with you Mister Power."

Unflustered, Johnny put a little star attitude into Gary's face.

"For Christ's sake Gary, just say it with the S."

Johnny ended the conversation right there and walked out of the arena.

Gary made a snide looking face from behind him as he left, mocking him by mouthing "Say it with the S."

He turned and burst into the locker room shouting, "Peace! You in here boy!"

Peace came out from behind a row of lockers.

"I'm here Mister Grasier."

"Man, I thought you were going to blow this chance. I bet you thought I wasn't going to make good for you Peacey baby, but here it is."

Gary opened the briefcase with the fifty thousand dollars.

"You kneeled and the whole world felt your pain. I couldn't have planned a better finish for that match myself. You could have one hell of a future in acting kid."

Peace looked at the cash in disbelief. Was Gary so dumb

that he believed it was acting? Gary shut the case and left it on the bench.

He pointed his thumb over his shoulder and said, "Now get out of my locker room kid. This place is for winners and you're stinking it up."

Gary turned on his heels and left the locker room. Peace looked down at the briefcase and then thoughtfully smiled.

Johnny headed straight for Grandfather's house. As he pulled into the driveway May Ling and Grandfather came out of the house in a rush. Johnny jumped from the pick-up's cab sensing there was something bad happening.

"Johnny, it is your mother," May Ling cried. "She is at the hospital. She's okay but we have to go."

"What? Why?"

May Ling reassured his concerns.

"She will be okay, I spoke to her on the phone. I told her we would get there as soon as you arrived. I'll explain on the way."

Johnny and May Ling climbed into the truck.

"Grandfather?" Johnny called.

Grandfather was on the porch and he called back, "I will only slow you down! Go!"

Grandfather waved them on. They sped off to the hospital. Along the way, May Ling did her best to explain what little she knew about what had happened.

They took the first and closest spot they saw in the lot and rushed in to find her room.

"Mom! Are you okay?" Johnny asked coming in the door.

Johnny pulled a chair up to the side of the hospital bed. Maria was actually quite comfortable, drinking a cup of tea and watching the soaps on TV.

"I'm okay Johnny. I just had a fright, that's all. The doctor asked to keep me for a couple of days for observation. I'm an old woman to them you know."

Johnny took her hand and asked, "What happened? Why did you get a fright?"

"I'll tell you all about it, but first let me give this beautiful girl a hug. Come here May."

She reached up and gave May Ling a warm welcome.

"You have been so good to my Johnny, I can't thank you

and your Grandfather enough."

May smiled and assured her, "I will give him your thanks when I get home."

Johnny was through with the niceties. He needed to know what happened and he wanted to know now.

"Mom, please! Tell what happened."

"Now don't go getting upset," Maria said. "There was a burglary at the house. I walked in while they ran out the back door and it startled me. I lost my breath and fell down, that's all."

"Did you see the people who broke in Mom? Did you get a look at their faces?"

She recalled the memory and thought for a moment and said, "Well, to tell you the truth, they looked like those people who fight on TV. They had on leather jackets, that's all I saw dear. I'm sorry."

Johnny was burned up with aggression but he didn't want Maria to see it. He changed the topic the best he could.

"I thought you were going to stay at the lodge for the whole week," he said.

"One of the girls was feeling a little homesick and wanted to come see her cats. We decided to make it a short vacation. Just silly, isn't it? She missed her cats."

Johnny smiled, hugged Maria and said, "At least you're okay."

She loved the attention and more than welcomed a hug from her son whom she loved more than anything at all.

"One more thing Johnny. Now don't get too upset," she told him.

"What is it mom?"

Maria found it hard to say, but he was going to find out soon enough. She might as well be the one to break the news.

"They took you father's Medal of Honor."

Johnny was aghast. He sat up straight, then stood up firm and leaned over to give his mother a kiss on the cheek.

"I really have to get going. I have to prepare for my next match."

"Don't you go looking for trouble now Johnny. You let the police take care of this."

Johnny gathered himself and stood at the foot of her bed.

"Don't worry mom. I had just gotten in when I heard you were here and I could use a shower, that's all."

"My goodness," Maria said. "I forgot about asking you how the matches were in all this excitement. Are you winning?"

"I've won every match so far Mom."

Maria looked happy with a smile on her face.

"You make me so proud Johnny."

He smiled with thanks and told her, "I'll come to see you after the last match tomorrow Mom. I promise. You can watch it on Channel Five, it will be televised."

"Okay. Good bye May," she said. "Please come back with Johnny."

May smiled and nodded. She adored Maria.

"Goodbye Mother Powers. I will."

Johnny and May Ling departed.

Grandfather watched Johnny frantically pace back and forth in the garden that afternoon. He was really upset about what happened with is mother and it showed. Grandfather was still and calm, watching him pace.

"This is not the key to enlightenment," Grandfather said.

"No! Kicking some ass is going to make me feel better though."

Grandfather shook his head disapprovingly.

"Right now you must put aside that angry emotion. Let go of what it is that makes you feel this way."

Johnny let out a groan of frustration.

"How can you tell me to just let it go. I'm so pissed-off right now I could tear any one of those jerks apart."

"Your vision is clouded with anger. Your strength is focused on the inside."

Johnny thought that he wasn't being heard. It frustrated him all the more.

"What are you saying?" Johnny demanded.

"I'm saying to breathe. Right now, you couldn't hurt another person. You are too angry. This is not why we learn to fight."

"You're telling me that I can't hurt a person? I'm burning up with energy here. I could just maul someone right now!"

Grandfather motioned him to stay put as he retrieved a practice board.

"You have broken one of these before?" Grandfather asked.

Johnny laughed and shot back, "With my eyes shut! Yeah!"

Grandfather held the board up and chest height and said, "This is your enemy. Strike them with all your aggression."

"Piece of cake."

Grandfather added, "With your eyes closed."

Johnny scoffed. He lined up his hand and drew back. As he released, he gave it an angry force and he hurt his hand on the board. It didn't break.

"Oh, ow! What the hell was that? A trick?" Johnny yelled.

"That was the end result of aggression. See, it gets you nowhere fast."

Johnny rubbed his knuckles and listened.

"You think that it is some power from within that makes you strong and you are right. Still, you must channel that power from within your soul. Deep inside, below your anger and below your feelings. There is a place inside of you that knows no boundaries. A place that will allow you to be the best that you can be. But anger is not the path to that place."

Johnny's temporary failure reset his thinking back into student mode.

"How do I find this place?"

"Breathe. Take a deep breath and you have taken the first step toward your enlightenment."

Johnny did as he was told and he breathed deeply. He continued to do so, with Grandfather's instruction.

"Root your feet into the ground and let the power of the Earth flow through your body. Move with the wind, breathe in the energy from plants and animals, flow with the water. From this place where you are, you can make your dream come true."

Johnny had his eyes closed and he moved his focus toward finding this place inside.

"I can be the best that I can be," he repeated to himself.

Johnny spent the next few minutes repeating this mantra and focusing on true power. Grandfather picked up three boards. He held them up.

"Do not open your eyes Johnny. Feel with your inner power and strike the target before you."

Johnny gathered focus. He drew his hand back slowly and held it there for another minute. His head swayed a bit as if in the wind and he burst out with a powerful strike. The boards shattered in the middle, splinters flew.

Johnny opened his eyes.

"You have entered a place that few of these so called Warriors today will ever know. This is the place where your soul will now find strength. Come. Now you will conquer all your shortcomings."

Johnny mastered the colored ring lesson. He stepped in and out of them while dodging and twisting around the barrage of tennis balls that Grandfather delivered.

At the sandpit he staved off the attack of the bamboo rods. One hand to each stick, and he never missed a block.

On the tennis ball machine, Johnny proved his mastery in

defensive blocking. They kept coming at full speed and Johnny struck each of them down. He jumped and connected with his feet. One after another, regardless of how he decided to block, strike or attack the oncoming objects, he never missed a one.

On the wooden man, Johnny was everything that his movie mentors appeared to be. He was swift like Jet Li and powerful like Chuck Norris. He moved with the speed of a Jackie Chan film and the accuracy of a military sniper, just like his father did during his service in the military.

Finally, sparring with Grandfather, Johnny was as limber and professional as Grandfather himself. Johnny felt that he had truly made the grade. Grandfather agreed.

Tomorrow would prove that one way or another.

Chapter 15

The next day parking was near impossible downtown. Even though the arena was two blocks off of the main street, the parking spaces were packed. Everywhere within a half mile of the arena were fans, radio and television crews and onlookers who just wanted to see a piece of the action.

Johnny, May Ling and Grandfather all enter the arena together. May had never seen anything like this before.

"Look at all the cameras. This is very exciting."

"Hey, there's Peace," Johnny said, pointing across the arena. Johnny called out and waved to get his attention.

"Peace, over here."

Over the noise and the bustle, Peace heard his name and came to meet Johnny.

"Ready for the big time?" Peace said excitedly.

"More than you know.," Johnny replied.

Peace smiled and gave a supportive shoulder pat. He said, ""I don't know how you can stay so calm."

Grandfather commented, "Perhaps one day I may show you how he does it."

He was interrupted by May Ling pulling him toward their seats.

Sheila and Gary were at their Owners Table surrounded by suit and tie personnel. They saw Johnny enter the arena.

"Your Golden Boy looks primed and ready," Sheila said.

"I have a plan that should take a little steam out of him," Gary said deceptively.

Gary waved to get Johnny's attention and beckoned him to come over.

"There will be two fights for you today Johnny," Gary told him. "There will be a little exhibition from The Punisher and we're going to have you up against Blade for a match."

Johnny shrugged in agreement.

"I'll take whatever you have Gary."

Gary smiled and said, "That's the spirit Hero!"

The Punisher came up behind Gary from the crowd of people rushing around. He addressed Johnny specifically though his black and white skull mask.

"Where do you want the flowers sent dork?"

Johnny fired back.

"You don't have to plan my victory party yet big boy, besides, you're not invited," Johnny shot back.

The Punisher was speechless, but Sheila wasn't.

"Feeling lucky today Johnny?" she poked.

Johnny turned to Sheila and threw her a snide look.

"So lucky," he said, "you can bet on it."

Sheila feigned an insulted look but she was truly surprised by his remark.

Johnny turned and left to return to his camp.

The Referee entered the ring and the cameras came to life. The announcer got on the microphone.

"Ladies and Gentlemen …"

Sitting together, Grandfather talked with Johnny at the bleachers.

"You have learned all you need to know for this fight.," Grandfather told Johnny. "Have faith in yourself and what is meant to be will be."

"I feel strong inside Grandfather," Johnny said. "I have no fears."

Grandfather nodded.

"I think The Punisher is coming out now," Peace announced, turning their attention to the ring.

The Punisher's opponent for the exhibition match was a Warrior Fight's regular named Stone. Like the punisher, he came out to the ring with a leather Lucha-mask on and colorful boots that matched his outfit.

"Now entering the ring, for the first fight today, Stone!"

The audience responded with yelling and cheering.

Suddenly the lights dropped. A green spotlight made a circle on the back wall of the arena.

"And featured in the first match of the day, the Champion of Warrior Fighting and the meanest man alive, The Punisher!"

As he came out of the doorway, lights flashed on and off and the crowd grew near riotous. With the grand display, the Punisher entered the ring.

Lights came back up as the two fighters squared off.

The plan for the match was to be a typical exhibition fight. While everyone knew well that The Punisher wouldn't be beaten, for the first few minutes of the match Stone would have the upper hand.

After a few turnbuckle tosses and some flashy kicking and striking maneuvers Stone was looking pretty good. Then The Punisher turned mean. He turned up the power and beat down on Stone's shoulders with heavy hammer-like blows. It was evident they were immediately taking their effect on him.

The audience didn't know better. It looked like the typical exhibition match from the Warriors, but Gary knew different. He watched as The Punisher's actions got unnecessarily violent and he repeatedly hurt Stone.

Gary rushed to the edge of the ring. He yelled in under the bottom rope, "For Christ's sake this is supposed to be an exhibition match."

Stone's body dropped down flat on the mat in front of Gary and he turned quickly to Blade waving him into the ring.

"Do something dammit! Do something!" Gary screamed.

Blade stormed the ring. He slid in under the bottom rope and sprang to his feet. He got right in between The Punisher and Stone.

The Punisher raised his arms and shouted, "You want it now Blade?"

Blade fired a clenched fist into The Punisher's face, sending him into a heap on the mat. Stone rolled out of the ring and was helped to his feet by two W.F.C. security guards.

The Punisher stood back on his feet, ready to fight. Blade slid back out of the ring shouting at The Punisher as he left.

"If you live today, I promise you a beating you will never forget."

Blade rushed over to aid Stone back to the locker room. Gary ran up to his side and grabbed his shoulder.

"You have a match!"

Blade pushed Gary back.

"Screw you and your exhibition matches. This man is a friend of mine and I'm going with him. Don't count on either of us to return."

Gary puts his hands up to plead but Blade just walked away. Gary turned to the Ref.

"Roll the big one!" he shouted.

The Punisher ran around the ring with his hands raised.

"Bring me Johnny Powers!" he yelled.

Johnny looked up at Grandfather, May Ling and Peace. Grandfather simply smiled and nodded. Peace shrugged his shoulders and May Ling blew Johnny a kiss.

It was time.

The crowd was chanting and feeding The Punisher's vanity.

Punisher! Punisher! Punisher!

The Punisher spotted Johnny at ringside and leaned over the top rope, pointing down at him.

"It's you man!" he yelled to Johnny. "You die now!"

Johnny just looked up at him, calm and collected. The Punisher reached into his shirt and pulled out the Medal of Honor. He waved it back and forth to taunt Johnny.

Johnny extended his arms and dropped his jacket from his shoulders. His body was ripped like never before. His adrenaline was pumping and he was ready.

Grandfather leaned over to Peace.

"It's time for Johnny to kick some ass," he said.

The Punisher stepped back to his side of the ring and hung the medal over the turnbuckle. Johnny bounded into the ring over the top ropes and raised the crowds chanting to an uproar of applause.

Voices were heard shouting things like:

"Fight!"

"Kill that mother!"

"Take him down Johnny!"

The announcer came over the in-house speaker system.

"Would everyone please calm down. Please ... thank you.

Tonight's fight card has changed."

The arena hushed.

"Now, Warrior Fights is proud to present, the highlight match you all came to see, the Rumble Royale!"

The Punisher stepped over to the announcer and commandeered the microphone.

"You want to get back your precious medal, you have to go through The Punisher to get it punk!"

He pointed to the Medal hanging from the ring post. Johnny shrugged his shoulders and lunged forward, driving a foot into the chest of The Punisher and knocking him completely off balance.

Completely surprised, The Punisher stood, dropping the microphone and readying for battle.

"Lets get this on," he shouted.

The Punisher returned a series of bashing blows as he came in on Johnny. Johnny blocked them but was forced back toward the ring's corner. When he reached the last foot of mat that he had to retreat on, he ran up the ropes and to the complete surprise of the Punisher, he jumped over his head removing his leather mask.

The audience gasped, then cheers rose from the stands. The Punisher shook his lengthy blonde locks out and regained his composure. If the secret of his face was out, he didn't care. All that mattered now was that Johnny would suffer and this just added to the list of reasons why.

As a back and forth battle of rage ensued, Johnny continued to give back equally as much action he took. It got long and started to wear on both fighters.

Johnny reached inside. He looked though the Punisher and saw the crowd behind him. He saw the thugs that harassed May Ling, the Warriors that trashed Lap's store and the hooligans that Peace had to deal with all the years of his youth. He saw the trials that Grandfather endured in his training and in the stands he saw May Ling watching him with anticipation. She looked worried and her concern transmitted to Johnny in the ring.

Johnny felt an animal inside. His focus was primed. His muscles throbbed with adrenaline.

With the roar of the crowd, and sheer determination, Johnny turned to face The Punisher. He looked at the monster towering over the ring and he dug his back foot into the mat.

Johnny exploded.

He delivered a beat down with precision and accuracy. He hit nerve points, pummeled joints and relentlessly attacked vital points up and down The Punisher's framework.

The Punisher dropped to his knees.

Johnny didn't let up like he did for his fight with Peace. He kept swinging. As The Punisher tried to stand, Johnny delivered strike after strike. When The Punisher got one knee up, Johnny kicked it out from under him. When he placed a hand on the mat to lift himself up, Johnny took it out and dropped him over and over.

With every bit of strength he had left, The Punisher launched his body up to get on his feet. As he tried to steady himself, Johnny left the mat and drove what has now become his signature strike. He brought down his straight right fist across The Punisher's forehead, raking his knuckles down the bridge of his nose. He was knocked him out cold before Johnny's feet landed back on the mat.

Johnny stood over The Punisher's body and the Ref ran in.

The crowd screamed and shouted at the ring. The fight was over.

At the side of the ring, Gary's mouth was wide opened in disbelief. Sheila belted him across the shoulder with her hand bag and she stormed off.

Warrior Fighters, office personnel and reporters rushed the ring. Peace ran down from the stands and squeezed through the pack of bodies and got in under the ropes. He grabbed Johnny's hand and raised it over his head.

A snapshot of moment made the front page of the newspaper the next day.

With The Punisher, still laying on the mat, Johnny walked over and took the Medal of Honor off the turnbuckle.

The Punisher's weary head opened its eyes and saw Johnny.

"My father had honor and he earned this medal. You got what you earned!" Johnny said to him.

Johnny stepped away from The Punisher as his weary head fell back to the mat. Reporters, cameras and Warrior Fights office people came to Johnny like a wall at ringside. They clapped and cheered.

Gary came out from the pack holding the Championship Belt. He stood before the row of cameras and addressed Johnny.

"Well Johnny, you did it! You earned the right to be the new Warrior Champion."

Gary held out the belt to Johnny. The crowd looked on anticipating his reaction. Johnny looked at it, then at his father's medal.

"I'd rather have honor, honestly," Johnny said.

Gary appealed saying, "Come on Johnny, you're the best. Wear our belt and prove it."

The cameras all focused on Johnny for his response. He took the belt from Gary's hand.

Gary said, "There you go Johnny. Now you're the best."

Johnny dropped the belt at his feet and stepped over it on live television.

"You're right," Johnny said. " I am."

May Ling jumped forward from the crowd and threw her arms around Johnny. Grandfather reached out and put his hand on Johnny's shoulder, guiding him out of the camera's watchful eye and toward the exit of the arena.

Gary watched his fortune walk away with a line of camera men behind him.

Chapter 16

Johnny was at the hospital to take his mother home from her ordeal. It was agreed that she would stay at Grandfather's house while the insurance company repaired her home. Johnny was ready to wheel her out to the car like a Queen.

"Did I tell you how handsome you look today Johnny?" Maria said.

"Thank you Mom. You look very beautiful too."

She reached back and touched his hand. Johnny stopped pushing her and came to the front of her chair to tell her something special. He couldn't wait any longer.

"I did get a medal after winning the match Mom."

She looked confused for a moment and asked, "Oh Johnny, I thought you turned them down."

"I did," he said.

He produced the Medal of Honor from his pocket. Maria started to sob.

"Johnny, you are your father's son," she said, welling up.

Johnny smiled with pride and said, "I wish he could have seen me today."

Maria consoled Johnny and said, "I bet he was right there beside you the whole time."

Johnny returned to rolling her down the hall. He wasn't finished with surprises yet.

"I promised you I would take the time to be your son mom. I meant it." he said.

"Johnny, that was just mother talk. You're a perfect son to me."

"Well, we're going to stay at the lodge for a week mom," he told her.

Maria perked up excitedly. "Johnny, you shouldn't have."

May Ling, Grandfather and Peace came around the corner of the hallway.

"You can thank Grandfather and May Ling. They set it up."

With a wide grateful smile, Maria looked over to May Ling.

"Sweetheart, you did that?" she asked May Ling.

May nodded with a smile and said, "Johnny has to keep his promises."

Johnny interjected.

"To be the best I son I can be."

Maria was joined in a hug by both Johnny and May Ling.

"My Johnny. You are the best you could ever be."

A Story By Joe Dolan

Chapter 17

Lap had his hands full in getting the General Store back together. It was coming along, but it still had a long way to go.

A knock at the front door brought Lap out from behind a row of shelves. The sign read 'Closed For Renovation', he didn't know who could be knocking.

"Hold on," he called. "I'm coming."

Lap opened the door to find a delivery man holding a box addressed to Lap Huon.

"Delivery for Mister Lap Huon," the driver said.

Lap looked at the box with curiosity.

"Sign here please," the delivery man requested.

Lap signed, said thank you and took the box inside. He cleared a space on the dusty counter and looked the box over. He shrugged his shoulders and grabbed for a mat knife to open it up and see what was inside.

As he got the cardboard off of it, he found it to be a briefcase.

He spoke to himself saying, "What is this?"

Putting his thumbs on the locks and his fingers on the sides, he snapped the latches open and stepped back just an inch.

Slowly, he took the front of the case in his fingers and lifted the top up wide. Staring for a few seconds, he started to smile and fainted backwards into a stack of empty boxes.

It was the fifty-thousand dollars.

17544894R00108

Made in the USA
San Bernardino, CA
13 December 2014